FALSE KNIGHT

*Peter Turnbull titles available from
Severn House Large Print*

After the Flood
All Roads Leadeth
Chill Factor
The Dance Master
Dark Secrets
Sweet Humphrey
Treasure Trove

FALSE KNIGHT

Peter Turnbull

Severn House Large Print
London & New York

This first large print edition published in Great Britain 2007 by
SEVERN HOUSE LARGE PRINT BOOKS LTD of
9-15 High Street, Sutton, Surrey, SM1 1DF.
First world regular print edition published 2006 by
Severn House Publishers, London and New York.
This first large print edition published in the USA 2007 by
SEVERN HOUSE PUBLISHERS INC., of
595 Madison Avenue, New York, NY 10022.

British Library Cataloguing in Publication Data

Turnbull, Peter, 1950-
  False knight. - Large print ed. - (The Hennessey and
  Yellich series)
  1. Hennessey, George (Fictitious character) - Fiction
  2. Yellich, Somerled (Fictitious character) - Fiction
  3. Police - England - Yorkshire - Fiction 4. Detective and
  mystery stories 5. Large type books
  I. Title
  823.9'14[F]

ISBN-13: 978-0-7278-7652-2

Printed and bound in Great Britain by
MPG Books Ltd, Bodmin, Cornwall.

Prologue

It was easy to kill, so the man had found, and given his profession, it was also, he discovered, surprisingly pleasant. He had enjoyed the power, much more intense than the power he had felt after taking his rape victims. How true, how true, he thought, that rape is a power crime: it is the thrill of disempowering someone, so totally, so completely; but much, much less powerful than the taking of life. That, he felt, was the ultimate, and it had indeed proved to be the case. Murder, he had found infinitely preferable, infinitely more fulfilling, infinitely more empowering. It was, though, much more short-lived than rape, because with rape, the victim was always out there, always alive, always damaged by him and him alone. The power he felt as a murderer was altogether different. Having taken life, it couldn't be returned to the victim. In respect of murder, there was the knowledge that he, and he alone, had snuffed out a life: someone's daughter, someone's wife, someone's mother, someone who was living one minute, planning her life ... and the next ... was not, all because of him. Unlike the rapes, the sense of power was short-lived, but oh, so intense. There was the further pleasure that he knew his victims, knew that their trust in him had been exposed to the ultimate betrayal, and that they knew they would soon, very soon, die. That look in their eyes, that fear, that resignation ... and how clever he had been, outwitting the police – that was all part of the game.

This last victim, the appropriately named Mary Golightly, for she had 'gone' with less resistance than had the others, had shared the same pattern as the previous victims. The relationship, the love affair, the talking about their future, when he alone knew that all would end in a dark and lonely place, as it had ended in a dark and lonely place in his last house. The romance, then the overpowering, the restraining with the length of chain. Then the calm explaining of what was going to happen – death by a massive blow to the head, any blood that splatters will be washed away with bleach, then the calm wait for a day or two until the blood in the body solidified, then the cutting up of the body, placing each part in a plastic bag, but ensuring the stomach had been punctured, because the body, in pieces, was going into the Ouse in weighted bags. The gasses in the stomach would cause the bag to rise, unless the stomach, and the bag, had both been punctured. The bags weighted with local stone or locally used brick that can be picked up anywhere, a rock here, a brick there, and then she is no more ... a missing person. Her clothing incinerated, all trace gone.

And that was how he had done it, except for one amazing blunder. Astoundingly, one bag had escaped notice. He couldn't drive back to the river, not now dawn was approaching. He saw wheelie bins at the side of the road; refuse awaiting collection later that day, having been put out the night before. He turned off the main road and entered suburbia, left his car and put the bag into a half-empty bin. It was one of the larger bags, it felt like her thigh. How could he have missed it? How could he? But it was still dark, those bins would be upturned into the back of the refuse lorry, they weren't done by hand any more, he'd be safe. The next one ... the next one he would keep alive a little longer. That was the mistake he had made with Mary Golightly. He hadn't kept her alive long enough ... but the next one ... the next one.

One

*in which a man of the old school searches for
'stuff' and in so doing launches a police
investigation.*

Larry Fenby was a cynic. He knew he was a
cynic. People told him he was a cynic. But
he'd been doing this job for many years,
right from the day the foreman had told him
to 'go ahead and waste the bins', which he
had interpreted as upturning the bins in
folks' gardens so as to 'waste' them, all to
the fury of the foreman and the glee of the
crew. Later it was explained to him that
'wasting the bins' meant tipping the contents of one half-full refuse bin into another
half-full bin, so as to give the crew one bin
to carry to the lorry rather than two. But he
had learned and had settled into the job,

and had grown to like it. He enjoyed being out of doors, he enjoyed walking the routes, he enjoyed the lifting and the carrying. He grew lean and fit and strong, and never once did he envy those who had to work in a factory for their pay, even in the winter when he and the crew had to battle through ice and snow and biting east winds. For domestic rubbish had to be collected. 'You are just as important as doctors in keeping disease out of York,' they were often told in their frequent pep talks by young suits and ties of the Department of Sanitation. He had joined 'the bins' when the job was messy, really messy, heaving metal tubs and tipping their contents into the back of a wagon, and when it was smelly, really smelly, and a cut to his hand could lead to a serious infection. He had stayed with 'the bins' when metal bins were phased out and householders put their refuse in plastic bin liners and carried them out on the eve of collection day. The use of plastic bin liners was preferable to the metal bins, he had found, but overnight, dogs and cats and foxes could do a lot of damage, and it became a common occurence for the crew, walking ahead of the lorry, to turn into a road and find the contents of the bin liners spilling out of the plastic. The crew wouldn't pick anything up save the bin liner itself, and so the team would leave refuse in their wake to be collected, eventually, by the street sweepers, who were seen by the 'bin men' as being of a lower status. Larry Fenby was still with the bins when washing facilities were introduced into the depot and the men could go home to their families after a shift smelling pleasantly of soap and aftershave. He was with 'the bins' when the environmentally hazardous bin liners were rendered safer by the introduction of 'wheelie bins', large plastic tubs on wheels into which the bin liners could be placed, with heavy enough lids to keep the cats and foxes out. The 'wheelies' would be placed outside homes on the relevant collection day. The specially-adapted lorry would arrive, by then the crew remaining with the lorry throughout, and special lifts on the vehicle would cause the 'wheelie' to rise and spill its contents into the rear of the vehicle.

At this time the crew were issued with light-weight overalls and efficient gloves so that at the end of the shift they were not physically tired, nor unpleasantly unclean, and Larry Fenby's waistline began to expand. He had been with the bins a long time. He had seen the Department of Sanitation become the Environment Department and he had become a 'professional' when his job title changed to 'Domestic Refuse Engineer', but being the cynic that he was, he would always describe himself as a 'bin man', or a 'dust-man'. Being a bin man of the old school, there was one practice he and a few other 'oldies' refused to abandon: the habit of scavenging. In the old days, when house-holders put out everything for the bin men to take away, a valued perk of a bin man's job was 'stuff'. Anything that was cast off by a householder, laid by the metal dustbin, was refuse, and seen as fair game by the crew. The crew were often motivated to do the round by the prospect of 'stuff' that they would find; useful off-cuts of wood; old, but still serviceable, tools; bicycles thrown out just because one wheel had become buckled; sets of golf clubs still good, but clearly having been replaced; items of furniture, chairs, stools, all in good condition, just needing a lick of paint or a coat of varnish. All was fair game and valued plunder for a bin man, and in those early days in Larry Fenby's working life, the lorry would return to the depot with refuse in the rear and plunder in the cab, with the crew observing the rule that any plunder belonged to the man who picked it up. As the service changed and washing facilities were introduced, as the Department of Sanitation became the Environment Department, as wheelie bins were introduced, the suits and ties who gave pep talks about the valued and important service done by 'Domestic Refuse Engineers' deemed that the practice of taking plunder should stop because it was 'unprofessional'. The issue of 'plunder' became a source of dispute, a strike was organized, the wheelies didn't get emptied, refuse mounted up, the cats became fat, and rats began to be seen. The local authority relented and turned a blind eye to plundering, and later countered by providing a collection service for any item that would normally have been put out with weekly refuse. Plundering therefore stopped, because all good 'stuff' was being removed to the city incinerator by the new collection service, whose staff were more youthful 'domestic refuse engineers', and keen to be 'professionals' and rise above the lowly practice of 'plunder'. Larry Fenby, however, had for many years softened his life as a dustman by means of 'stuff', and was not, as he approached retirement, about to give up the practice. He had, as a consequence, developed the habit of peering inside wheelie bins before they were lifted into the back of the lorry. That was how he found the human thigh.

It was placed on top of the contents of the bin, wrapped in a black plastic bin liner, tightly bound with masking tape. That, he thought, was unusual, as was the shape. It just looked like the shape of a human thigh. He took his penknife and cut open the plastic, and revealed what was unmistakably human flesh. He stepped back. A ghost from his past came to the forefront of his mind. He could keep it quiet, just let the stuff be tipped into the back of the wagon and the suits and ties wouldn't know he'd been plundering. He knew that he wouldn't be dismissed for doing so because the union was too strong, but he'd be earmarked for early retirement or 'natural wastage', which he didn't want, he couldn't afford it. The ghost, though, was that of his brother who many years earlier had disappeared, just walked out to the pub one evening and had never been seen again, leaving his family and relatives in a permanent state of not knowing what had happened to 'our Henry'. And here, in front of him, was a part of a human being which had clearly been cut up to be disposed of in a way that it would never be found. Here was somebody whose family would already be missing him or her, and knowing the torture of not knowing. Larry Fenby, the plundering cynic, chose to raise the alarm.

Nicola Butterworth awoke. She felt well. She had a clear head. It was really going to be one day at a time. 'Try not to look too far ahead,' had said the kindly worker at the addiction unit. 'One day at a time, even one hour at a time, but don't look beyond tomorrow. The reward is waking each morning knowing you had a dry day the previous day. You'll feel better, healthier, your appetite will return, as will your self-respect.' She found it to be true. The irony though, the irony, moving to York to look for a better quality of life, only for *that* to happen to her. She basked in the sunlight as it streamed into her bedroom ... the irony ... the irony.

George Hennessey slowed his car as he approached the crime scene, as a crime scene it unmistakably was, the area cars with their blue lapping lights, the unmarked car driven by Detective Sergeant Yellich, the SOCOs taking photographs, and clearly using flash, despite a high sun on a cloudless day. He parked behind the black, windowless mortuary van that had been summoned, as procedure dictated, whether corpse or body part, whatever 'it' was, 'it' had to be removed in the mortuary van. The driver and his mate glanced uninterestedly at Hennessey as he walked past the vehicle in white shirt, summer jacket and a comfortable panama, slightly misshapen with age. He stooped beneath the blue and white police tape and approached Yellich.

'A leg,' Yellich said, after the courtesies and greetings had been exchanged. 'Or part thereof.'

'Part?'

'So I was told.'

George Hennessey wiped his brow and glanced about him. A few members of the public stood a respectful distance from the police tape, gathered in ones and twos, but this was Dringhouses, modest owner-occupied homes of the upwardly mobile, whose houses were burgled because there was something to steal from within, who liked the police in their neighbourhood and whose children were always home on time. If this were Tang Hall or Osbaldwick, or other similar areas of the famous and faire, then the residents would be pressing up against the police tape with mouths agape with curiosity, as often, thought Hennessy, people once stood, mouths agape, at public executions.

'A thigh. Found in this wheelie bin by the bin men, or bin man.' Yellich consulted his notebook. 'By one Lawrence "Larry" Fenby. He was looking for booty.'

'Naughty,' Hennessey smiled.

'Yes, indeed, very frowned upon by the city fathers, but fortunately he did it.' Yellich paused. 'He said he thought it didn't look right, so he slit the plastic liner with his pocket knife, saw what he saw, and told his boss, who phoned in to the police on his mobile. Scene of Crime Officers are just finishing up now.'

A camera bulb flashed.

'Flash!' Hennessey sighed, 'On a day like this? Hot and going to get hotter.'

'Dare say they know what they're doing, skipper.' Yellich smiled. 'The bin lorry and crew left. No reason for them to stay. I've got a note of Mr Fenby's address. He seems an honest man, despite the tendency to moonlight, and he was also candid enough to tell us we'll find his prints on the plastic.'

'His, and his alone, I'll be bound.'

'I think so too, sir. The bin belongs to the

household at thirty-two Bingham Walk. That's ... that's the house there, yellow door.'

Hennessey looked to his left. He saw a neatly-kept house, neatly-kept garden, and a very alert and neatly-kept Springer spaniel sitting on the threshold of the half open door. 'Had a rummage in the bin liner...'

'A rummage?' Hennessey frowned. 'I'm sure you didn't.'

'Well, not a rummage, sir. I know better than that, but there was a utility bill next to the leg, had the address of thirty-two Bingham Walk.'

'Ah ... have you spoken to them yet?'

'Not yet, sir.'

'Well, when you do, or whoever does speak to them, better advise them of the dangers of identity theft. It's a growth industry, as you know.'

'Indeed, sir.'

'And these?' Hennessey glanced along the line of wheelie bins standing at the gates of the houses along Bingham Walk.

'I asked the bin men to leave them, sir.'

'You did?'

'Well, yes, sir, there's a thigh in one, a human thigh ... there's no telling what's in the others.'

Hennessey smiled and nodded. Yellich was correct; again, youth was on the ball. It was one of those instances which he found happening with increased frequency and which led him to believe that his retirement was approaching at the right speed and at the right time. 'Quite right. Quite right.'

Yellich looked pleased with himself. 'Just waiting on Dr D'Acre now, sir. She should be here anytime.' He glanced at his watch.

'She's here now.' Hennessey smiled and indicated to his left.

'Ah, yes.' Yellich followed Hennessey's gaze and watched as a red and white Riley RMA approached the collection of police and other official vehicles and halted behind Hennessey's car.

'Lovely old lady.'

'Don't let her hear you say that!' Hennessey glared at Yellich.

'I was ... I was actually referring to the car, sir.'

'Oh, I see ... sorry ... yes, it's a lovely old

machine. Older than you ... sadly not as old as me. I remember them being launched, just as I came out of the Navy. They were what today would be called an "instant hit", but were out of the pockets of most folk. When the machines appeared we still had German and Italian prisoners of war clearing the streets of snow and ice, and rationing was still in force.'

'Really?'

'Yes, really. Don't know why we held on to the Italians but the Germans, they were Germans who came from Eastern Germany, sending them home after they had been "tainted" by the West into a Stalinist state was to send them to certain death, or long-term imprisonment at the very least. Some of the Germans settled in the UK, others went to Canada, the States, New Zealand, Australia, South Africa ... Rhodesia, as it then was.'

'I see. Well, thanks for the history lesson.'

'Yes, the UK after the war was one very large transit camp, a right mess, and in the winter of 1947 when Dr D'Acre's lovely old lady was built ... well, that's another history lesson for another time.' Hennessey turned and smiled and greeted Dr D'Acre. A slender woman, with short, close-cropped hair, she wore no make-up other than a trace of pale lipstick and displayed good muscle tone and excellent poise by the way she walked, carrying what Hennessey knew to be a heavy Gladstone bag. Yellich similarly smiled and nodded.

'Gentlemen.' Dr D'Acre inclined her head. 'What have we got?'

'Female,' Dr D'Acre said upon being shown the thigh. 'Can't really age it other than to say that, as you see, it's neither very young nor very old, not child nor geriatric, but somewhere in between ... but you don't need to be a pathologist to see that. The leg has been dismembered from the body by sawing. This is not a dreadful accident of the kind one hears about ... of a severing of a limb. This was carefully sawn from the torso. See, you can make out the striations in the cross section of the bone, caused by the teeth of the saw.'

'Yes,' Hennessey growled.

'The blood is clotted.' Dr D'Acre turned

to Hennessey and their eyes met briefly before she rapidly turned away. 'This man or woman or team knew what they were doing. They let the blood solidify before dismembering her. No blood-soaked crime scene for you on this one, Chief Inspector.' She waved the flies away. 'The plastic wrapping has prevented the flies getting to it until just now, otherwise we would have had some notion of when it was placed here.'

'Last night.' Yellich smiled. 'The bins were placed outside last night by all the householders on this estate. I checked.'

'I see ... so, you're saying that someone came along last night and lifted the lid of one bin at random and placed this item inside?'

'Seems so, ma'am.'

'Well, it's certainly possible. Heavens, if I don't recover my bin after our weekly collection, it gets filled up with other folk's rubbish, half-eaten pizzas and empty cans. Better than littering the streets, I suppose, keeps the vermin down. But to the matter in hand. She was well nourished in life and was Caucasian. I can't really gauge her height ...

the bone was sawn above the knee, which means that the femur is cut through. With this part of the anatomy, I would need the whole femur to be able to offer an estimation of her height. I could offer a very wide guess, but it would be a guess.'

'Well, at this stage, ma'am,' Hennessey said, 'anything would help us.'

'I'll have it transported back to the lab. It won't be a post-mortem, I can't tell the cause of death from this. I mean, assuming she is dead. It'll take a lot more than the loss of a leg to make death a certainty ... the owner could still be alive. Terrible thought. But I think we can assume death, the solidifying of the blood indicates thus, if nothing else. The veins and arteries are full, which they would not be if this were an amputation. Some blood would be lost in an amputation.'

'Yes ... I think we can assume death too.' Hennessey's jaw set firm. 'And the bits of her ... the other bits will be, well, they'll be where they'll be.'

Dr D'Acre snapped on a pair of latex gloves and probed beneath the flesh and the bin liner. 'This is interesting,' she murmured.

'What have you found?'

'A brick. No, two bricks. Now, why would someone want to wrap a thigh in a plastic bin liner together with two house bricks?'

'To immerse it,' Yellich offered. 'To make sure it stays under water.'

'Has to be.' Dr D'Acre continued to probe. 'More your department than mine, but it has to be. Hate to encroach, but his plan went awry.'

'Oh, encroach all you like.' Hennessey wiped his brow, and stepped back from the bin. The stale smell was rising. 'All help gratefully received.'

'Well, as Sergeant Yellich said, the bricks offer no purpose other than to weight the leg. So something didn't go according to plan. For some reason, he didn't drop this into the river or the estuary or out at sea from a motor launch. I imagine, though, but only imagine, that is where the rest of her will be: in some deep, vast body of water. But that is for you gentlemen to pursue. I think I have taken this as far as I can here;

I'll take an air temperature and then have the thigh transported back to the lab at York District. I'll send the bin liner to the forensic laboratory at Wetherby. If there's anything of interest on or in the bag, I'm sure they'll find it. I'll send the bricks, too.'

'If you would, thank you.'

'What will you do now?' Dr D'Acre put the thermometer back in its leather case, having taken a note of the reading.

'Search through all the bin liners, though I doubt if we'll find anything, if as you say, she was cut up and destined for the deep.'

'I don't doubt it too, but I dare say it has to be done.'

'Indeed it has, and a house-to-house.'

'That might be more profitable.' Dr D'Acre knelt and closed her Gladstone bag. 'I mean, some person or persons unknown put it there. Well.' She stood. 'I'll come back to you a.s.a.p. with anything I can tell you about the thigh. I'll extract DNA, which will be useful; essential, in fact. It's the only way you'll be able to identify the person, unless you find the head in one of those bins.'

'Which,' Hennessey sighed, 'as you said,

we won't.'

For the remainder of the day it was basic police work, a fine attention to detail, a leaving of no stone unturned. With two police officers to each wheelie bin, the contents of which were tipped unceremoniously on to the pavement and then carefully, item by item, replaced in the bin. The search, the sift, was carried out under the watchful eye of a uniformed sergeant. Hennessey and Yellich split up and called on each house on Bingham Walk and in the adjacent streets besides, careful not to tread on each other's toes by agreeing that Hennessey should call only on the even numbers and Yellich, 'the odds'. It was Yellich, walking Bingham Street, who struck gold. After a succession of unanswered doors which were noted and listed for a 'revisit', and after a succession of, 'Sorry, didn't see anything. What's happening anyway? They say a body's been found, is that true?', Yellich finally received the reply he'd been yearning for.

'Probably. Might have done. In the night, about dawn. Yeah, reckon I did see something, something peculiar. Didn't think it looked right.' Yellich thought the owner of the voice to be a teenager, about seventeen or eighteen, male, short black hair. He wore a yellow leisure shirt and white slacks. He had a thin face. Yellich thought he seemed nervous.

'What did you see?'

'Hardly anything.'

'Just tell me.'

'It was dark, about four a.m. I was up, couldn't sleep, was looking out of my window.'

'Four a.m.?'

'Yes. About. Saw a man walk down the road, then he walked back. Then he drove away.'

'So he walked towards the wheelie bin, over there?'

'Towards where they found the body, yes.'

'Then walked back?'

'Yes.'

'Then drove away?'

'Yes.'

'Did you see the car?'

'No, but it was a big expensive car. Didn't hear it arrive, didn't hear a door open and shut. Only sound I heard was the sound of the wheels on the road ... made a soft hissing sound. No slamming of a door, no engine noise, no gear change ... that's an expensive car. Nobody round here drives anything like that.'

Yellich thought it a fair point. He nodded as to encourage the youth. 'Tell me about the man?'

'Tall. Wore dark clothing. Had a hat. He walked normally. I mean, wasn't running, just a normal walk. The only reason I looked at him was because he was the only thing moving, and because I didn't recognize him. I've grown up here. I know everybody round here, not to speak to, but I know them. I would recognize a stranger ... and he was a stranger. But he wasn't carrying a dead body. They say a dead body's been found.'

'Never mind what "they" say. Was he carrying anything?'

'Just a bag.'

'A bag? What sort of bag?'

'Like a sports bag, but smaller.'

'A holdall?'

'Yes,' the youth nodded. 'A holdall. Nice bags. He carried it there and was carrying it when he walked back. A dark bag.'

'Any writing on the side?'

'None, just a plain bag. Seemed fuller on the way to the bins, no weight on the way back. You can tell if a bag is full or not, or whether it's heavy, by the way they're held.'

'Yes, yes. So there was something in the bag on the way from the car?'

'Yes. The straps were taut and the guy leaned away from it as he walked and his arm was straight ... the bag also looked full, it had more shape to it.'

Yellich smiled, the youth's statement reminded him of the joke: a wife complains to her husband that he is 'not in shape', to which he retorts, 'Yes I am, round is a shape.' But he knew what the youth meant: it is evident when a soft material bag is full or not. 'Could you put an age to the man?'

'Old ... sixties. It's difficult, it's summer now, but it's still dark at four a.m. He wasn't under a street light, could have been younger.'

'How old you think I am?'

'Thirties...?'

'All right, good enough. So, sixties ... but could be younger?'

'I'd say.'

'All right.' Age, Yellich knew, was difficult to assess, and meant little. As a young constable he was once called to a disturbance in a pub, and had been astounded to find that the man who was getting the better of the other man was an astounding seventy-nine years old. Yellich had seen older-looking men in their fifties. 'Clean-shaven, bearded?'

'Seemed clean-shaven.'

'Seemed?'

'Well, no huge Santa Claus type of beard, that's for sure, but I was too far away to say clean-shaven for sure. I mean, he could have had a pencil-line moustache or a closely-trimmed beard. So I can't say clean-shaven for sure ... just being honest.'

'Fair enough. Now ... clothing. What was he wearing?'

'Nothing particularly unusual, male clothing, male summer-time clothing. Had shoes which clicked, like his heels had metal tips...'

'That's interesting.' Yellich wrote on his notepad.

'Hard soles at least, definitely not carpet slippers. Not all folks' shoes make that tapping sound as they walk. Especially men. Most men walk silently.'

'Spend a lot of time at your window, do you? Sorry ... what is your name?'

'Francis. Francis Beale. People call me "Frankie".' He smiled.

'All right, Frankie, so you spend a lot of time at your window?'

Frankie Beale shrugged. 'I suppose I do, I don't need much sleep. I'd prefer to sit watching the world go by my window than watch cable TV. Been like it for a long time. Don't want to take knock-out drugs.'

'Good for you.' It was, thought Yellich, a mature response. 'So ... his clothes ... his shoes had a hard sole, possibly with metal tips. What about his trousers?'

'Light-coloured, light brown, summery trousers.'

'Top?'

'Jacket, again, a summer sports jacket.

Hat, a flat cap, but a posh flat cap, more like a golfer's flat cap than a coalminer's cap.'

'This is helpful.'

'Really?' Frankie Beale glowed with pride.

'Oh yes. Do you think you'd recognize him again?'

'I think I would. You want me to call you if I do?'

'Yes...' Yellich dipped into his pocket and extracted his mobile phone and selected a pre-dialled number. 'Hello. Yes, this is DS Yellich, attending the incident at Bingham Walk. Can you put me through to the collator, please.' He looked at Beale. 'Get a crime number for you to quote if you see this fella again. Yes, collator, DS Yellich. Do we have a crime number for the incident at Bingham Walk? ... It was reported today. Wait...' He rested his notebook against the wall and wrote, holding the mobile phone to his ear by trapping it between his ear and left shoulder. 'Got it, thanks.' He folded the phone shut and then, having pocketed it, he took a calling card from his breast pocket and wrote his name and 16/06 on it, and handed it to Frankie Beale. 'There you are.

Still not ten a.m. when it was reported, and it's already the sixteenth reported crime of the month.'

'Blimey.' Frankie Beale looked at the card as though it was a valued possession. 'You're DS Yellich?'

'Yes.'

'Interesting name.'

Frankie Beale was clearly losing his nervousness, and Yellich liked him for chatting freely. He was evidently a youth with nothing to hide from the police. 'Yes, Eastern European, but many years ago, many, many, many years ago.'

'So, I ring this number and ask for you, sir?'

'Yes. And if I am not in, ask for CID in respect of crime number 16/06, saying you've seen the man again. We really want to talk to him. He may have had nothing to do with the ... the incident, but we want to eliminate him. If we can.'

'Well, like I said, pretty well every evening I'm at my window. I haven't seen him before, though, and somehow I doubt if I'll see him again. But if I do ... yes, I'll call.'

'Are you employed, Frankie?'

'A student.'

'Student?'

'Yes, at the university, but I don't want to leave home ... so I went to the university here, eventually.'

'Eventually?'

'Well, I had a gap year. Or two.'

'How old are you, Frankie?' Yellich was genuinely curious.

Frankie Beale smiled. 'Older than I look. I can still get away with asking for half-fare or half admission fee but I'm twenty-three, twenty-four soon.' He held up the card. 'But yes, I'll phone if I see him.'

Tony Beevers had been a police constable for a little over twelve months and, like all 'new' constables, found himself posted to the enquiry desk, it being seen by the senior officers as a valuable learning experience. Each member of the public who comes in has a different query or complaint, each phone call likewise, and on long periods when the city is quiet and callers few, valuable time can be used reading police manuals and large textbooks. In those twelve months, PC Beevers had come to be able to assess each caller to the bar upon first sight either as 'friendly' or as 'trouble', and sometimes humorous in its own way, as with the drunk who wandered into the police station and who, not having committed a crime and not at all disorderly, had done so because he often found himself inside one when in his cups. Consequently, having downed twelve pints of strong beer and six double whiskies, he could think of nowhere else to go but the police station, such was his strength of association between drunkenness and the police. Tony Beevers had, on that occasion, simply turned him round and pointed him in a homeward direction. He pondered the wisdom, or otherwise, of his decision for the remainder of that shift, but the man was not brought back into the police station by patrol officers, there was no reported disturbance in the city that night, and Tony Beevers had seen him in the street a few days later, looking trim and slender and well turned out.

Phone calls, he had found, were also like

that. Sometimes the phone had an insistent quality about its ringing tone; sometimes an instinct would tell Beevers that this call was 'friendly' or 'trouble'. Perhaps it was the news that a leg had been found in a dustbin in Dringhouses which influenced him; perhaps it was because he hadn't been phoned by 'trouble' for a few days, but for whatever reason, when the phone on the desk behind the enquiry desk rang, Tony Beevers knew it was trouble. He laid the ballpoint pen in the centre of the legal text he was reading, turned and picked up the phone. 'Police, Mickelgate Bar, PC Beevers speaking.'

'It's that woman.' The voice was female, timid, shaking, it seemed to Beevers.

'What woman, madam?'

'The woman in the house opposite. This is the right police station for Gravely?'

'Gravely? Yes, yes we are.'

'Well, it's that woman. They're always fighting, them two, always at each other's throats ... now she's gone. She was last seen on Friday, and he was seen leaving the house in his car, fuming with temper, then not a squeak from that house all weekend, and now it's Monday and no one has seen her since Friday. Well, he's done her in, hasn't he? Fed her to the pigs. Plenty of pigs round here, no better way of getting rid of a body, my husband used to say. A pig will eat anything if she's hungry enough ... so said my husband, and he worked the land all his days and he said if he ever wanted to bump someone off, he'd not feed a herd of pigs for a day and then put the corpse into the pig-pen. It would take less than half an hour for a herd of hungry pigs to eat, and there'd be nothing left, not even the bones. A pig's jaw can crush a skull, so my man said. Then you'll eat him or her.'

'The pigs?'

'No ... well, yes ... see, if the pig eats a human and you eat the pig ... well, no one's seen her.'

'Can I have your name please, madam?'

'Oh no ... no, can't have my name, oh no.'

'Well, what is the name of the lady whom you suspect is missing?'

'Not suspect, son, she is missing. I suspect he's done her in at last, always threatening to.'

'All right ... her name?'

'Mary Golightly and she lives at fifteen Atlas Crescent, Gravely, Yorkshire.'

'North,' Beevers said to himself as he wrote down the address. 'Gravely is in North Yorkshire.'

'Well, that's it,' said the quavering voice. 'I've done my public duty. It's up to you now, but that house has never been so quiet.' The caller put the phone down.

'Thank you for your information,' Tony Beevers said into the empty phone. He replaced the handset and then picked it up and dialled the switchboard. 'Hello.'

'Switchboard.'

'Enquiry desk. Can you trace that last call by 1471?'

'If I can, I'll come back.'

'Thanks.'

Beevers replaced the handset a second time and began to write the content of the call and the details provided on a referral pad. He was still writing when the phone rang. He picked it up. 'Enquiry desk.'

'Switchboard.' The voice had a serious,

humourless tone. 'She didn't shield her number. I checked the reverse directory for you. The caller was Michael Platt ... listed as Michael Platt.'

'She indicated she was a widow.'

'Probably is ... just kept the phone in her husband's name. Anyway, she lives at twelve Atlas Crescent, Gravely.'

'Twelve? Well, that suggests credibility. She was phoning about a woman at number fifteen ... bang across the street. This is something the CID. should know about. Thanks.'

George Hennessey drove out to Gravely. He had returned from Bingham Avenue with one or two addresses that still had to be visited noted, with Yellich's possibly useful interview with Francis 'Frankie' Beale in mind, and with the police officers making a detailed search of the wheelie bins. He had bolted a hurried lunch in the canteen, which was contrary to his usual practice, had returned to his desk as his phone rang. He listened to PC Beevers's account of the call he had just received from Mrs Michael

Platt, and had said, 'All right, Yellich's still occupied, I'll drive out there myself,' and replaced the handset with a sense of resignation. He avoided driving whenever possible.

Hennessey had never been to Gravely before, and even though the village had a through road, and was evidently larger than nearby villages, it still seemed to him to have a sense of isolation about it. The through road clearly wasn't very busy, and seemed to Hennessey to go from nowhere to nowhere across flat countryside, with the squat village of Gravely halfway along its length.

'But I never gave my name, sir,' said a shocked Mrs Platt. 'My address either. I never gave either.' She was a frail, pale-looking woman with silvery hair, and was probably younger than she appeared. Her house was a drab-looking cottage, probably council owned, observed Hennessey, and was so small that she fitted tightly in the doorway.

'We traced your call,' Hennessey explained.

'You can do that?'

'Yes.' He smiled. 'It was quiet when you called, our switchboard operator dialled 1471, got your number ... any member of the public can do that. If you want to conceal your number, you have to dial 141 in front of the number you are going to ring.'

'Well...'

'But you can't do that from a public callbox and you can't conceal your number and then dial the emergency services ... well, not a 999 call anyway.'

'Well ... but that would only give you my phone number. How did you find my address?'

'We, the police, have reverse telephone directories, all the numbers are in numerical order rather than names in alphabetical order ... a member of the public can't do that. So, you have concerns about your neighbour?'

'Yes ... you'd better come in, sir.' She stepped back and Hennessey bowed his head and shoulders and then twisted sideways to enter the woman's cottage. It was not, he thought, dissimilar to what it must be like to enter a doll's house. In the main room he couldn't stand fully upright without his head touching the ceiling.

'They're not big houses, are they, sir? You'd better take a seat.'

'Well, I've been in bigger.' Hennessey sat gratefully in an armchair which was clad in a cream covering, decorated with a pattern of red roses. He glanced about him and read 'rural self-respect': no signs of wealth, but the brass was polished, as was the wood, and the house was clean and neat.

'I'm used to it. I'd get lost in a big house. Been here all my married life. We got married when I was twenty, had a week in Scarborough in a bed and breakfast, and then we got the bus home and we came into this house, through that front door, hardly anything in it then, a few sticks of furniture. We built it up over the years, as my man worked on the land, mostly for Mr Conway. He's the biggest farmer, but once in a while for others, but he went back to Mr Conway. Two bedrooms upstairs, a scullery and kitchen and a privy out the back.'

'You have an outside toilet?'

'Yes, but it's got proper flushing water.'

'Good. Well, tell me about your neighbour.'

'Oh,' Mrs Platt lowered herself into an armchair. 'Well, she's in the posh house.'

'The posh house?'

'There, across the road. See, when we first moved in here, and right up until about twenty years ago, we used to look out across fields, and then Mr Conway sold some land to a builder who built those posh houses on the other side of the road.'

Hennessey looked through the small front window of Mrs Platt's cottage and saw spacious-looking detached houses with angled brown-tiled roofs. They were brightly painted and would be designed to appeal to middle-income families who could get more for their money if they were prepared to move out of York, so assumed Hennessey.

'We didn't like the idea at first, looking out on to a row of houses, didn't like it when they were being built, it was like our village was being invaded. But afterwards my man quite liked them because he didn't have to spend evenings and weekends looking at where he'd be working the next day. He found he could escape from the fields a bit more. In his head, I mean.'

'Yes, I know what you mean. You sound as though you are by yourself now.'

'Yes, Michael passed over a few years after those houses were built.'

'I'm sorry.'

'He had a good life. He got married, was a respected farmhand, had two sons and saw them grow up and he met his grandchildren and died in his sleep. I woke up next to his body. He had a good life. So I do not feel sorry for him. Now Mrs Phillips, two doors down, her man...'

'Yes, yes.' Hennessey held up his hand. 'So tell me about Mrs Golightly, the lady who lives across the street.'

'Well ... those two, always rowing, arguing, argue, argue, argue, him shouting, her screaming back at him, things being broken, like crockery being smashed ... could hear them across the street. I'd sit here and listen to them. Sometimes Mrs Phillips was here too and we'd hear them and look at each other and say, "They're at it again," and Mrs Phillips would say, "Haven't they heard of divorce?" You see, her regret ... with her man...'

'Yes.' Again Hennessey held up his hand. 'Just tell me about the Golightlys.'

'Well, Friday last they were at it again. She left the house, then a bit later, about half an hour later, he left in his car, same direction, towards the village centre. That's the last I saw of her.'

'So why do you think something ... or some harm has come to her?'

'Haven't seen her over the weekend. Fight like cat and dog, they would, but she'd always still be there, both would still be there. You see, one day Mrs Forbes from next door was with me and Mrs Phillips and we heard them, and I said, "They're at it again," and Mrs Phillips said her usual, "Haven't they heard of divorce?" and Mrs Forbes, she said, "Divorce? Not them. Murder, yes, but divorce? Never."'

'So you think she's been murdered?'

'Well, she's not to be seen. He's pottering about like nothing has happened, but she's not been in that house since Friday evening, early. That's just not like her, she's always there.'

'I see.' Hennessey spoke softly. 'I see.'

'Just concerned, I was. Not getting nosey, but she hasn't been there since Friday.'

Hennessey stood. 'Well, thank you, Mrs Platt. I'll go pay a house call.'

Feeling Mrs Platt's eyes on him, and doubtless, he thought, the eyes of Mrs Phillips and Mrs Forbes as well, Hennessey stood at the kerb of Atlas Crescent and waited as a John Deere, driven by a strapping, stripped-to-the-waist lad, drove powerfully by, and then strolled across the road and down the drive of number fifteen. He pressed the doorbell, which he found had a harsh, continuous sound that stopped when he released the button. Wired to the mains, he reflected; not his preference. His own home had a battery-operated bell which gave a softer 'ding dong' sound, and which would still work in the event of a power cut. The door was opened slowly, casually, by a middle-aged man in a younger man's clothes. He didn't, thought Hennessey, suit the T-shirt which said 'Malta' over an outline of the island, and his legs, at his age, really needed summer slacks, not shorts, and his feet needed shoes, any shoes at all. He just hadn't the feet to go barefoot, but then, in fairness, he was in his own home, and would not go into the village like that. He blinked at Hennessey. He wore heavy-framed spectacles and had combed his few strands of hair over the top of his head to cover his balding. Hennessey thought it looked silly. So called 'comb-overs' were a source of irritation to him.

'Yes?' The man held the door wide. He was much smaller than George Hennessey, yet showed no fear of him.

'Mr Golightly?'

'Yes?' He was thin-faced, an old scar on the right side of his forehead.

'Is your wife at home?'

'No.' He shook his head. His eyes were steely cold.

'Do you know where she is?'

'No. And you are?'

'The police.' Hennessey showed his ID. He watched for a reaction on the man's face. There was none. No startled look in the eyes, no jolt of fear. No reaction at all.

Nothing. Certainly nothing that Hennessey was hoping to see.

'How can I help you?'

'By telling me where your wife is.'

'I haven't reported her missing.'

'Someone else has.'

'I thought the next of kin...'

Hennessey shook his head. 'Nope ... anybody can report anybody as being a missing person.'

'Oh ... even so, I didn't think the police investigated missing adults.'

'We don't, as a rule. But when there is clear suspicion surrounding the disappearance of someone, then we do.'

'And there's suspicion surrounding Mary's disappearance?'

'Seems so.'

'Are you sure you're a policeman? I thought plain clothes bobbies visited in pairs.'

'We are short staffed. My sergeant's up to his ears on another enquiry, this seemed like something one man could do, just taking a statement, in the first instance.'

'So why is Mary's disappearance of interest to you guys?'

'Well, because you and she were arguing. She was seen walking out of the house, you were seen to drive after her, and she hasn't been noticed round your house over the weekend.'

'Those old crows across the road. Living in a village, nothing is sacred. You'd better come in.' He stepped aside.

Hennessey stepped across the threshold. The house had a musty smell, particularly of newsprint, which had been left in the sun in a room without opened windows. He glanced down the hall to the kitchen and saw an uncleared table and a pile of un-washed dishes in the sink. The house was, he thought, untidy, but not necessarily unclean. It reminded him of his own home just after the second of his life's tragedies, before he had a 'help'.

'Yes, it's a bit of a mess,' Golightly read Hennessey's mind, 'But she'll clean up.'

'She?'

'Mary. Do you want to go through there, that door?' He pointed to a lilac-coloured door to Hennessey's left. Golightly stepped forward and held it ajar.

'Thank you.' Hennessey pushed the door fully open and walked into a neatly kept room. Nothing was out of place, though the air was a little stale. Hennessey thought it a room used only to entertain, or for other special circumstances.

'You're not at work today?' He asked.

'No ... I can work from home on the computer. I can do anything at home that I can do at the office, hell of a lot more relaxing too. Dislike jackets and ties and the importance of walking smartly past the boss's office carrying a piece of paper at least once a day.'

'Yes, I see you go for the casual look.'

Golightly smiled. 'Well, I wasn't expecting visitors. Take a seat.'

Hennessey sat on an armchair, sank into it, he thought, with deep sides and soft cushions. The thing seemed to swallow him. Golightly sat opposite him in a similar chair.

'Did you intend to report your wife as being a missing person?'

Hennessey glanced about the room. There were prints on the wall showing urban scenes, a mirror over the fireplace, a bowl of plastic fruit on the windowsill.

'Possibly.'

'You don't seem concerned about her.'

'I'm not.'

'Has she done this before?'

'Not for this length of time. I'd be lying if I said otherwise, and anyway, those crows over the road have told you that she's always home, which is an exaggeration, but she's most often here.'

'So why would you only possibly report as an MP?'

'Because she might only possibly be missing. She's always threatening to go and live with her sister. She might have done it this time.'

'You haven't checked?'

'No.'

'Do you often argue?'

'Yes.' He glanced towards the empty fireplace. 'It's been like that for a while. We're just too old to separate and find someone else, I suppose. I suppose we've just got used to arguing, well, fighting. If we stopped, we wouldn't know what to replace it with. It's the way we are.' He paused. 'I like the silence.'

'The silence?'

'Of the empty house. On Friday evening, and all through Saturday, I was re-fighting the argument over and over in my head. Then on Sunday morning I woke up and thought, "This is quite nice". I've discovered the house can be peaceful. It's nice. I need a woman for the cleaning and the washing, of course.'

'Of course.' Hennessey echoed.

'But I can hear myself think for the first time in years.'

'So she left on Friday? Did she take anything with her?'

'Don't think so.'

'So when she goes she usually goes away for...? How long would you say?'

'A few hours. Once or twice she's been away overnight, so those crows across the road aren't really accurate. They just don't know when she's at home or not. But two nights ... and a Monday ... she'll be at work. I dare say she'll be at work. So I am not worried.'

'Where has she stayed when she's been out overnight?'

'Don't know and I don't care.'

'Where does she work?'

'She's a receptionist at the health centre.'

'Small number of employees?'

'Suppose. Health centres don't employ many people.'

'So, she'll be missed?'

'I suppose she would.'

'They haven't phoned to enquire about her?'

'Maybe, but I've been on the machine all day. It blocks the phone line.'

'I see. You drove away after she left the house?'

'Yes.'

'Where?'

'Just drove. Clears my head after an argument. The crows across the street could have told you that there was nothing unusual in that.'

'I see ... so, shall we see if your wife's at work?'

'The computer's still on.'

'I'll call in when I leave here.'

'If you like. Can't miss it, right next to the pub. Appropriate, you might think.'

'You mean the medical conditions created by alcohol?'

'Yes.' Golightly smiled. 'A bit like the sculpture of a bottle outside Teesside Crown Court. I mean, all those people who end up in the dock because of taking a drink too many; very appropriate to have a sculpture of a bottle outside the courthouse, isn't it?'

'Dare say, haven't really given it much thought. Do you have a photograph of your wife?'

'Why?'

'To save me calling back if she is not at work. If she is at work, I'll explain my reasons for calling and give her the photograph.'

'There's a recent one upstairs.' Golightly stood.

'I wonder if I could go up with you?'

'Why?'

'I'd like a sample of her hair.'

'Why?'

'Again, to save me coming back if she is not at work.'

'But her hair?'

'Just a strand or two from her hairbrush. We can obtain her DNA from it, if she's not at work. If she is, I'll give her hair back to her and she can destroy it, so she knows we don't have her DNA on our database.'

'If you wish.' Golightly turned and left the room and took the stairs with a speed and agility which surprised Hennessey. Moments later he returned with a photograph, which showed a woman in her late thirties, auburn-haired, a round face, warm eyes.

'It's a very pleasant photograph,' Hennessey offered.

'Aye, well, it was her sister that took it.'

He handed Hennessey a hairbrush. Hennessey turned it upside down; a few long hairs were caught in the comb.

'They're all hers,' Golightly said. 'She's the only one that uses that brush.'

Hennessey peeled a few strands of hair from the brush and placed them in a self-sealing cellophane sachet.

'Do you always carry those little bags?' Golightly asked.

'Yes.' Hennessey smiled his reply. 'Many

big cases have been solved by little bits of evidence.'

'So I hear.' Golightly's voice had a sarcastic edge that Hennessey hadn't noticed before. 'Well, if that's all? I have work to do.'

'For the time being.'

'For the time being?' Golightly shot a glare at Hennessey. 'What does that mean?'

'It means for the time being. If Mrs Golightly is not at work, it means we have a mystery on our hands, a mystery of a lady who disappeared in suspicious circumstances.'

'An argument!'

'Yes. That's suspicious enough. Well, we'll be back if Mrs Golightly is not at work.'

'If she's not at work, she'll be somewhere. With her sister, most likely.'

Hennessey looked again at the photograph. 'How tall is Mrs Golightly?'

'She's short. A little over five feet tall.'

'Yes...' Hennessey nodded. 'Well, I'll call in at the health centre. Back towards the village, you say?'

'Yes. That way.' Golightly tossed his thumb over his left shoulder. 'Past the pub.'

Hennessey returned to his car, turned the vehicle round in a neat three-point turn, and drove slowly towards the health centre. He had been a police officer all his working life, save for two years in the navy as a National Serviceman, and in his years of service, he had developed an instinct, an intuition, which he would often refer to as 'his waters'. On that pleasant summer's day, 'his waters' not only told him that Mary Golightly would not be at her place of employment, she would not be anywhere else, but his 'waters' also told him that a bit of Mary Golightly, to wit, her thigh, had been found earlier that morning in a wheelie bin by a dustbin man seeking to enhance his income.

He drove back to York, pleased to leave the village of Gravely behind. The village had an atmosphere, a character, that he didn't at all take to. The receptionist at the health centre had been cheerful, but distant at the same time, as if observing company policy to be warm and welcoming to all patients and visitors, but seeming to Hennessey that she was really wishing she was somewhere else, with someone else, doing something else. 'No, sorry,' she had said, 'Mary's not in today. Twice the work for me, we work the reception area together. No, she didn't phone in sick and yes, it's very unusual for her, never done it, in fact.'

Upon his return to Micklegate Bar, Hennessey sent the hair sample by courier to the forensic laboratory at Wetherby, 'reference crime number 16/06'.

There was little else to do then but wait. He sat back in his chair. The hair would identify the body part found in the wheelie bin as being that of Mary Golightly, and her husband would prove to be her murderer. At least, he thought, as he glanced at the sunlight streaming through the window into his office, at least, this one would be closed quickly.

'This feels naughty.'

'Naughty?' Hennessey smiled.

'Well, it's a bit of an immature word, but it's the only one I can think of.' Louise D'Acre drove her 1947 Riley RMA along the narrow lane, occasionally brushing the vehicle against the foliage. 'It's like playing truant.'

'And who didn't play truant when at school?' Hennessey rested his arm on the open window of the passenger door but kept his shirt rolled down, mindful of the article he had once read about doctors in Australia who couldn't understand why so many men were presenting with skin cancer on their right forearms, until it was realized that it was caused by the practice of car drivers steering their car with their left hand, with the window down, while resting their right arm on the car doorframe and not feeling the heat of the sun because of the breeze caused by the car's speed.

'Well, I didn't. Mind you, girls' grammar school, straw hats and white gloves and starched blouses ... all very proper. Truancy was unheard of at my school.'

'Not so mine. Trafalgar Road School, Greenwich ... rough school, doesn't exist any more, got knocked down to make room for a block of flats. Pity, really.'

'Pity? Why say you?'

'Well, probably it was sensible planning,

but it means I can't ever revisit a significant building in my life. I wasn't particularly happy there but it still was a significant building for me.'

'Yes ... I know what you mean. When I go home to Middlesborough, I can't help looking at my old school if I should drive past it, or indeed the house in which I grew up. So, yes, I know what you mean.'

'Colomb Street is still there, can't see them knocking those houses down ... not for a while yet. The old street has hardly changed at all, in fact, just an awful lot more cars and no extra room to park them ... and Trafalgar Road ... that's pretty well gridlocked from nine to five.'

Louise D'Acre slowed the car as she approached a village. It was, Hennessey saw, a very neat settlement with a clean and closely-cut green within a white-painted boundary, a duck pond, and the sadly almost inevitable war memorial. The detached houses lining the main road were proud-seeming, tidily kept and clean.

'Never been here,' Hennessey remarked.

'A colleague recommended it.'

'What is it called? Remind me.'

'Wheatley Priory. The Priory is a ruin now, I understand. The pub ... it serves lunches all day, so it's not really truancy, we're just knocking off a little early ... the pub is at the far end of the village as we have approached it. Keep a weather eye peeled for the Pack Horse. This road is apparently an old pack horse route ... hence the pub's name ... and the lunches therein are exquisite ... again, so I am told.'

'Here!' Hennessey indicated the pub ahead and to the right. The pub sign hung in the still air from a green-painted post. The pub itself seemed old, to Hennessey's interested but untrained eye. He saw it to be a large, bold-looking building, and it reminded him of Louise D'Acre's house, whitewashed, brilliant in the sun, with the exterior timbers picked out in black gloss paint.

Louise D'Acre and George Hennessey strolled arm in arm through the heat haze, which shimmered above the surface of the car park, and into the welcome cool of the interior of the Pack Horse. Hennessey escorted Louise D'Acre to the restaurant area where he asked the polite, young, eager-to-please waitress, for a table for two by the window.

'You want to watch the village go by?' Louise D'Acre asked as she slid gracefully into her seat.

'Just an old copper being an old copper.' He smiled as he consulted the embossed menu.

'Ah ... and I thought by phoning you and suggesting a discreet rendezvous I would have the pleasure of receiving your undivided attention over a late lunch.'

'And you shall ... but if my eye happens to be caught...'

'I will understand.' She slid her hand across the table and squeezed his. 'Just teasing. Well, the fish casserole for me, I think. Sounds delicious.'

'Me too ... mouth-watering, as you say.' He glanced around him: solid furniture, deep carpets, other diners eating slowly in almost total silence, the main lunch business of the day having clearly by then departed. The Pack Horse and Wheatley

Priory did indeed seem to be quite a find.

At the conclusion of the meal, which they both declared 'excellent', Louise D'Acre excused herself as Hennessey ordered the coffees. As he sat alone at the table, his eye was drawn to a couple who walked out of the building and across the car park to a silver Citroën C4. Hennessey, with a police officer's eye, observed them. The man was in his late forties, at a guess, neatly groomed, short black hair, clean-shaven, sports jacket, cavalry twill trousers, brown brogues. He looked to Hennessey to be very much in place at the Pack Horse Inn. His partner was younger, much younger, wearing a long blue summer dress, and as she walked she eyed the man with admiration. No reason for Hennessey to be suspicious, but in the absence of Louise D'Acre he wrote down the car registration number, more to give himself a sense of completeness than for any other reason. He pondered the possibility that he would be jotting down observations well into his retirement. Once a copper, always a copper.

'Strange how death unites us, isn't it?'

Louise D'Acre slid onto her chair. 'I was thinking ... I mean we are not united by death, that's the wrong way of putting it, but our jobs ... the way we met ... do you remember? That young man with the interesting knife wound?'

'Yes ... yes, I remember ... you invited me over to the table to take a closer look ... it was the first time we made eye contact.'

'And body contact. Our fingertips touched.' She smiled warmly.

'Yes...' He returned her smile, equally warmly, and this time he slid his hand across the table and took gentle hold of her hand. 'This has been one of those lovely lunches that has gone far too quickly ... but I feel united with Jennifer still ... her death hasn't separated us.'

'It won't ... clearly such a loss for you, but it won't be a separation.'

'Yes,' he held eye contact with her. 'Imagine ... twenty-three years old, just a few months after Charles was born ... just walking in the centre of Easingwold, shopping for her family ... people thought she had fainted, but she was, as is said in medical

65

speak, "life extinct".'

'Yes ... it's still a medical mystery, SDS. Sudden Death Syndrome. No warning signs, no symptoms ... no indication of cause of death. I have done post-mortems on victims of SDS and all were in perfect condition ... all young, in their twenties; it seems to strike the young adult, and there is nothing ... nothing at all to indicate why life suddenly leaves them, nothing to point us in any one direction. Fortunately it is rare ... very rare, so rare that a grant to study it can't be ... won't ever be, provided.'

'But she approves of us.'

'You think so?'

'I know so. I talk to her each evening, as soon as I return home, just me and Oscar ... and her. I scattered her ashes in the garden at the back of the house, the garden she designed ... and I told her about us, and I kid you not ... I felt a glow, a real warmth which could not be explained by the sun's rays alone. It was ... mystical. Very beautiful. She more than approves of us ... I know that she is happy for us. She was a very gener-ous-spirited woman. Ah...' He leaned back as a smiling waitress approached their table with the coffee.

She had rapidly lost all track of time. The blindfold was total, utterly efficient, letting in not a single glimmer of light. Just one meal thus far, cold, bland. No sound either. The cotton wool and the ear defenders saw to that. It was cold. It was the summer of the year, a hot summer too, yet the floor was cold, so cold.

Two

Tuesday, 2 June, 10.00 hours – 14.12 hours
in which the prime suspect is interviewed.

The polite, reverential tap caused Hennessey to look up from the papers on his desk. A fresh-faced, nervous-looking constable stood on the threshold of his office. 'Yes?'

'Courier brought this, sir.' He approached and handed Hennessey a buff-coloured envelope.

'Thank you.' Hennessey extended his hand and took the envelope. 'Haven't seen you before.'

'No, sir. PC Best, sir. First day was Saturday, sir.'

'Good man, welcome aboard.'

'Thank you, sir.'

'Just out of probationary year?' Hennessey opened the envelope.

'Yes, sir. Did my probationary year up at Northallerton. Then was posted here.'

'Well, hope you find us well.'

'Thank you, sir. Will that be all, sir?'

'Yes, thank you.' Hennessey extracted the contents from the envelope. It was a report from the forensic laboratory at Wetherby, reference crime number 16/06 of this year. The scalp hairs provided a perfect DNA match with the tissue samples sent from the pathology laboratory at York District Hospital.

'Blimey.' Yellich looked at the document after Hennessey had called him into his office. 'That was quick, a result in less than twenty-four hours. Solemn.'

'Well, they don't operate a queue system, thank goodness. Very recent murders are given priority, cold cases have to wait, and we only gave them one sample to check against one other sample. It would have given a junior technician something to do in order to settle into the rhythm of the day. But yes, they're very good, nonetheless.'

'So, we know the identity of the owner of the thigh. Nothing else was found in the bins, by the way, boss.'

'I was going to ask ... but yes, she was Mrs Mary Golightly, unhappily married and in a constant state of hostility with her husband.' Hennessey told Yellich of his call to the Golightly household.

'He didn't make a favourable impression on you, boss?'

'Well...' Hennessey reached for the file marked 16/06 on his desk and wrote in felt-tip pen by the number, 'Golightly, Mary'. 'It's hard to say what I thought of him. He didn't seem too upset by his wife's dis-appearance and made no secret of their volatile relationship, but he couldn't claim they were happily married, not with the evidence they had, "the crows", as he called them.'

'The crows?'

'Three elderly ladies who live opposite him. Not a single household ... I mean, three elderly women who are neighbours.'

'I see.'

'His wife was seen to leave the house ... that was the last time she was seen by an independent witness.'

'Do you mind?' Yellich pointed to the chair in front of Hennessey's desk.

'No, please, I'm sorry, I should have asked you.'

'So,' Yellich slid onto the chair. 'So, she was seen walking away from the house?'

'Yes.'

'Rather puts her husband in the clear, I would have thought, sir. Well out of the frame.'

'Don't let's jump too rapidly. In the first place there is a strong motivation ... the marriage was just poisonous. Murder your spouse to avoid an expensive, messy divorce. That's an age-old motivation, old as crime itself, and played equally eagerly by both men and women. She was seen leaving the house; it does not mean that she did not return. Also, he was seen leaving the house in his car about half an hour after she had left, going in the direction that she had gone, as if driving after her. We just don't know what happened that night, and is that night relevant? That was last Friday. Dr D'Acre has still to come back to us with her findings but to my untrained eye, that flesh, not nearly one week old when it was found...' Hennessey paused. 'She, Mrs Golightly, was not seen in the house over the weekend, but that doesn't mean to say she wasn't there.'

'Of course.'

'So, as always, we look at the in-laws before we look at the outlaws.'

'Anything known, boss?'

Hennessey tapped the phone. What were the results of the criminal record check, that was what Yellich meant by that question. Yellich knew he should already have looked into the Golightlys' background. And he hadn't; he'd forgotten. 'Waiting for the collator to come back, shouldn't be a minute or two ... that's if either are known to us. Accessing the Police National Computer will take a little longer.'

'Of course.' Yellich stood. 'So I presume we're going to bring him in?'

'Yes. Today.'

'Right. If you can give me ten minutes, boss?'

'Yes, I'll collect you.'

'Thanks, sir.' Yellich left the room.

He was 'slipping', 'going off', 'losing it', whatever term he cared for, it was him. Forgetting to do a CR check. Inexcusable, and the young constable, what was his name? Best. Looking at him in awe as though the older, the wizened and wise should know all the answers. Again he thought that he was clearly approaching retirement at the right time. He leaned forward and picked up the phone on his desk and angrily jabbed a four-figure internal number.

'Collator!' The voice at the other end of the line was crisp, efficient.

'DCI Hennessey.'

'Yes, sir.'

'Can you do a criminal record check, please?'

'Yes, sir.'

'Mary Golightly, late thirties, early forties. Her address, fifteen Atlas Crescent, Gravely.'

'Gravely? That's a local address, sir.'

'Yes. It's in our patch.'

'Very good, sir.'

'And check her husband too.'

'Do you have his first name and numbers?'

'No. You can get his first name from the voters' roll, his numbers ... I'd say he's mid to late forties.'

'Very good, sir. If we haven't anything, I'll access the PNC.'

'Yes, if you would, thanks.' He replaced the handset. He sat back in his chair resignedly. Not inviting Yellich to sit, not doing a CR check ... and the worst thing, the very worst thing, was that he knew Yellich had known that he had forgotten to do the CR check, and he knew that Yellich knew he knew. Yellich's diplomacy in letting Hennessey think he had done the check, his 'Anything known, boss?', rather than the less diplomatic, 'Have you done the checks?', and his allowing Hennessey to save face by returning to his desk on some pretext so as to allow said check to be done. He thought himself indeed fortunate in his Detective Sergeant. Very fortunate indeed, but Hennessey also felt a sense of frustration in that Yellich seemed to be so much more on the ball ... so much more on top of it all. He felt a lessening of his grip. He stood and glanced out of the window of his office at the medieval walls of the ancient city, glistening in sunlight, and walked by a throng of foot passengers, tourists in the main, with brightly coloured clothing, sunhats and cameras, walking in pairs or in groups, interweaving with one another, the walls not having a one-way system. Occasionally he recognized a local, a man or woman who didn't look to left or right as they walked, and who walked with a purpose in their step, on their way somewhere, and knowing that the easiest and speediest way to cross the city is to 'walk the walls'. He turned away from the window as the phone on his desk rang.

'Hennessey.'

'Collator, sir.'

'Yes?'

'Nothing known of anybody of that name or address.'

'Thank you.'

'If you can obtain dates of birth, I'll check with PNC.'

'Yes,' Hennessey nodded, 'I'll get that

information to you.'

He replaced the phone and walked briskly to Yellich's office. 'That was the collator.'

'Anything, boss?'

'Nothing. Let's go and bring him in.'

Maurice Walls pondered his neighbour, a quiet man, he would nod 'hello' but otherwise would keep himself to himself but that was the way of it anyway in Vicarage Lane. The man reminded Walls of another man he had once known ... a wealthy man, a man who had a house and nearly an acre of garden – and what did he do but take an allotment? People who don't have gardens take allotments, not fellows with more than enough land surrounding their house. It was a lock-up in this case. His neighbour had a good-sized house, yet he rented a lock-up on the edge of the village. It was definitely him: Walls had seen the car and its owner outside a lock-up, door open, not once or twice but numerous times when driving past. It was as if his neighbour valued the rundown lock-up for some reason...

★ ★ ★

The red recording light glowed softly. The twin audio-cassettes spun slowly.

'The time is eleven fifteen a.m., Tuesday, second of June.' Hennessey broke the tense silence in the interview room. 'The location is Interview Room Three at Micklegate Bar Police Station in the city of York. I am Detective Chief Inspector Hennessey. I am now going to ask the other persons present to identify themselves.'

'Detective Sergeant Yellich.'

'Rupert Croy, solicitor, of Croy, Wilcox and Wilcox, present under the terms of the Police and Criminal Evidence Act, 1984.'

Golightly glanced at Hennessey, then he said, 'Terence Golightly.' Short, simple.

'Mr Golightly, you have been arrested in connection with the murder of your wife, Mrs Mary Golightly. Do you wish to offer any information?'

'No.' Golightly was dressed in the same casual manner in which he was dressed when Hennessey had called on him the previous day. He stared intently at Hennessey, and, thought Hennessey, was clearly a very angry man, and a man with a short fuse.

'Except that being accused of murder is no way to break the news to a man that his wife is deceased. I shall be complaining.'

'That is your right.' Hennessey paused. 'So, when did you last see your wife, Mrs Mary Golightly?'

'Friday, last Friday. She left the house. I know there are witnesses to that.'

'Yes, there are, there are also witnesses who state that you were seen driving away from the house in the same direction that your wife took, as if going after her.'

'There's no other way. If my wife was seen going towards the village, that's because that was where everything is, shop, pub, bus stop, and if I drove that way, it was by co-incidence.'

'Where did you drive?'

Golightly shrugged. 'Just drove. It cleared my head after the argument.'

'You argued a lot with your wife, we understand?'

'Well, you understand correctly. Doesn't mean to say I killed her. It was just the nature of our marriage. My parents argued like that, all the time, but Father still wept at

Mother's funeral.'

Hennessey took his gaze from Terence Golightly and glanced round the interview room, the polished tiled floor, the hessian wallpaper, the various shades of brown, light and dark, that was the colour scheme of the room; the table, the four upright chairs, an opaque window which let in natural light, though the principal light source was a filament bulb concealed on the ceiling behind a perspex shade. He had to concede that Golightly had a valid point: an ever-arguing couple might, in their own way, still be very much in love. 'You didn't report her missing?'

'No, I didn't.'

'When did you expect her to return?'

'Monday ... well, Sunday evening.'

'So, when she leaves home, she stays out for two evenings?'

'Sometimes.'

'Where does she go?'

'Haven't a clue.'

'You must have some idea.'

'Her sister's, then. It's the only place she can go.'

'Who is her sister?'

'Meryl Ryan.'

'Address?'

'She's here in York ... on the Rawcliffe estate, Reighton Street, number twenty-seven.'

Hennessey noticed Yellich write the name and address on his notepad.

'She didn't return on Sunday evening. Were you not at least a little puzzled?'

'No.'

'She didn't return by Monday...'

'Clearly.'

'Still not worried?'

'No. We've been married a long time, I know her, ought to, and she's a survivor.'

'She was a survivor. Whatever happened to her, at whoever's hand, was something she couldn't survive.'

'Again, clearly.'

'Even by Monday forenoon you still had not reported her missing or made enquiries about her.'

'No.'

'Because you knew she was dead?'

'Please ask all questions clearly, Chief

Inspector.' Rupert Croy raised his eyebrows from behind his steel-rimmed spectacles. '"Because you knew she was dead" is an accusatorial statement, an attempt to put words into my client's mouth. Could you rephrase that last remark? Please.' He was a man in his forties, slender, smartly dressed.

'All right. Why did you make no enquiries about your wife's whereabouts when she was so late returning home? Why didn't you report her as being a missing person?'

'Because, because, because.' Golightly sighed. 'I knew my wife to be one of life's survivors. She can ... could take care of herself.' He paused. 'And because ... as I said to you yesterday, I was getting to like a quiet house. The appeal was growing rapidly on me. I even got to the point where a part of me was hoping that she wouldn't return.'

'So you won't be weeping at her funeral, as your father wept at his wife's funeral?'

'No. I make no secret of it. The marriage had failed long ago. That's still a long way from saying that I killed her.'

'Do you know of anyone who'd want to harm her?'

'No.'

'Which, you must admit, brings us back to you, Mr Golightly.'

'Inspector ... please.' Rupert Croy again raised his eyebrows.

'What do you do for a living, Mr Golightly?'

'Is that relevant, Chief Inspector?' Once again, Rupert Croy looked at Hennessey over the rim of his spectacles.

'We don't know what is or is not relevant at this stage, sir. It's a valid question.'

Croy glanced at Golightly and nodded, 'You can answer that question.'

'This and that.'

'Please be more specific.'

'I work for a food distribution company. I work in the distribution side, that's why I can work at home, so long as I have a computer. With the computer I can do everything at home that I can do in the office.'

'Always worked there?'

'No. It's a new company, Bielby Foods. About ten years old.'

'Bielby? Is that the name of the owner?'

'No, it's the name of the village where it is

situated. The owner is a man called Heinz. There's already quite a large food company called Heinz. You might have heard of it?' Golightly smiled at his own humour.

'Yes ... so what did you do before you joined Mr Heinz at Bielby Foods?'

'I was in the retail meat trade. A butcher.'

'Really?'

'Yes, really. Doing well until the BSE scare stopped everybody buying beef. Just could not make the shop continue to pay when folk stopped buying beef. There's more profit in beef, you see. Profit margin is different for each type of meat; hardly get a penny profit on chicken, but a Sunday joint of beef ... the king of meats. It was beef sales that kept High Street butchers afloat. The BSE scare meant a lot of people avoided meat altogether. My father was a butcher and he well remembers cows getting the "shakes", as they were called. Couldn't give milk, and so it would be slaughtered and the meat sold to butchers.'

'Into the human food supply?'

'Yes. Didn't harm anybody. Nothing new about BSE; it's just recently been identified, but it's always been with us.'

'I see. So you have butchering skills?'

'Yes.'

'You'd know how to cut up a human body in the most efficient way?'

'Yes.'

Rupert Croy once again glanced over the top of his spectacles at Hennessey, but made no comment.

'Your wife was dismembered.'

Golightly's jaw dropped. His face paled. The silence in the small room was almost audible.

'Oh...' Golightly groaned.

Hennessey was disappointed in the man's reaction. If he was feigning surprise, it was a very convincing act. Hennessey suddenly realized that he might not have his man after all; it might be that this inquiry was going to be far more long and complex than he had thought it would be.

'You break the news to me that my wife has been murdered by accusing me of her murder...'

'Of suspecting you.'

'It's the same.' Golightly snarled the

words.

'Not quite.'

'It feels the same. Accusing, suspecting ... not a great deal of difference if you are the accused, if you are the one under suspicion. Now you tell me she was ... cut up...'

'Yes. I'm afraid so.'

Golightly sank back in the chair. 'You mean it was her that was found in a dustbin? I saw the television news.'

'Yes.' Hennessey nodded. 'That was Mrs Golightly.'

'How do you know if there was only her leg?'

'The DNA taken from the leg matches the DNA taken from the strands of hair in your wife's hairbrush. Unless another person used the hairbrush?'

'No, no...' Golightly shook his head slowly. 'Only Mary used that brush. Those were her hair strands. Nobody else's.'

'Very well. There is, therefore, no doubt that the leg was that of your wife.'

'Could she still be alive? I mean the rest of her?'

'No. Our pathologist examined the leg

at the scene. She noted that the blood in the veins and arteries had solidified. That happens twenty-four to forty-eight hours after the heart stops beating. So she is deceased.'

'Am I suspected? Still?'

'Yes,' Hennessey spoke firmly. 'It was a violent marriage, verbally at least, if not in other ways.'

Golightly glared at Hennessey in a manner which said clearly that the Golightly union was certainly violent in other ways, emotional, physical...

'She was last seen a few days before her leg was found and, like I said, it takes a few days to allow the blood to solidify.' Hennessey spoke slowly, solemnly. 'And you have butchering skills. You would know how to cut up a human body. The leg had been sawn. Not hacked. Sawn. A butcher would know that a leg has to be sawn: hacking is messy. And a butcher would know that blood has to be drained off or allowed to solidify in order to prevent it spilling every-where. So, yes, I am afraid you are a suspect. Motive, means and opportunity, it's all there. So where did you do it?'

'Chief Inspector!'

'Where? Do you have access to other premises we don't know about?'

'Really!' Croy slapped his palm on the tabletop. He turned to Golightly. 'Don't answer that. Don't respond at all.'

Golightly smiled at Croy. 'Thanks, but I want to answer it.' He turned to Hennessey. 'Yes, you are right. I didn't do it at home, and I didn't do it in the lock-up I rent, because I didn't do it at all. I didn't do it in the first place.' He held his hands up in front of his face and turned them round as if inspecting the palms and the back of his hands. 'There is blood on my hands ... but only animal blood, animals that were slaughtered for human consumption. I was a slaughter man once.'

'Slaughter man, butcher, manager in a food company...'

'Always been in the meat industry one way or another. Do all sorts of other food now: meat, fruit, vegetables. People think that being in food is safe work.' He shook his head. 'It isn't. People think that, well, folk have to eat, so food is a safe business to get into, and so food companies are always opening and closing again: competition is fierce. I'll tell you something about food products. The fancier the packaging, the less substantial will be the product.'

'I'll remember that. So, where did you drive?'

'Drive?'

'Last Friday evening. You left your house in your car and drove away, about half an hour after your wife walked out. Where did you go?'

'Out towards the coast.' Golightly shrugged. 'Just followed the road.'

'Take on petrol anywhere?'

'No. Left with a full tank, came back with half a tank.'

'Pity.' Hennessey leaned forward in his chair.

'Why?'

'Well, if you had refuelled, you would have been caught on CCTV. Handy things, those CCTV cameras, provide evidence and alibi in equal measure. A lot of resistance when they were introduced; now the public sees their worth.'

'Haven't stopped crime, though.'

'They were never intended to. Just makes it more difficult to get away with. So, tell me about the lock-up.'

'It's where I keep the old lady.'

'Let me guess ... a car, has to be a car, a Rolls Royce?'

'I wish. No, it's a Jaguar Mark Nine, built in 1959. Hasn't got a scratch on her and less than fifty thousand miles on the clock. That's genuine. Well, I haven't wound it back, anyway.'

'You don't run it?'

'Again, I wish ... the insurance ... well, I'll leave you to guess.'

'Why keep it, then?' It wasn't a question that had any relevance to the inquiry, but Golightly was beginning to open up and Hennessey wanted him to talk. 'I mean, it's a bit like vintage wine: can't drink it, why collect it?'

'For the same reason that people collect vintage wine. As an investment. Better return than putting your money in a building society, but only if you are prepared to take a risk, because the classic car market goes up and down. I mean, the rises and falls in the classic car market are unbelievable, a real roller coaster. Right now it's depressed. Just six months ago, I could have sold the old lady for four times what I'd get for her now. So in the lock-up she stays.'

'We'll have to look in there.'

'Be my guest. The only female in there in whole or in part was made in Coventry in the last century.'

'Thank you, we'll take you up on that. And we'll have to search your house too.'

'Why?'

'Just routine. This is a murder inquiry.'

'Doesn't really answer my client's question,' Croy said dryly.

'With respect, Mr Croy, it's not for your client to ask questions, but I will explain. The house and the lock-up are probably crime scenes, and we cannot leave any stone unturned. So where is the lock-up?'

'Behind the post office in the village. There's a row of garages, you know the type, concrete built, upwardly hinging metal door.'

'I know the type.'

'Well, mine is number three in the row.'

'Number three?'

'The key is hanging up in the kitchen at home, marked "lock-up".'

'Couldn't be easier.' Hennessey paused. 'So your wife was employed?'

'Yes.'

'And she has a sister?'

'Yes, and a brother. He's in the south though. Portsmouth.'

'I know it well. Or knew it.'

'Nice city.'

'Yes. It was anyway. I stepped off a destroyer there at the end of my National Service, which, like your old lady, belongs in the last century.'

Golightly smiled. A change, thought Hennessey, a relaxing of awareness. If he did murder his wife, this is when he'll let something incriminating into his responses. He decided to ease off the pressure.

'Doubt he'll be in the Andrew though? Her brother, I mean.'

'He isn't, he's a bank manager. They

should be told.' Golightly appealed to Hennessey. 'I forgot about them.'

'You didn't phone them to let them know their sister was missing?'

'No, and I haven't had a chance to phone them to tell them she's no longer with us.'

It was a fair point. 'I'll send a constable to see your wife's sister. We can phone, often we do, but we prefer the personal touch.'

'She lives in York, as I said.'

'I have the lady's address, sir.' Yellich tapped his pad. 'Shall I go and see to that?'

'If you would, thank you.' Hennessey reached for the 'off' button and said, 'The time is eleven forty-seven a.m.; the interview is suspended to allow Detective Sergeant Yellich to leave the room.' He pressed the button. 'Would either of you two gentlemen care for a coffee or a tea? Machine vended, I'm afraid, but it's all we can run to.'

'Not for me,' Croy sniffed. 'Thank you.'

'Me neither.' Golightly tried to sniff at the offer in the same manner as Croy, but he hadn't the background and the gesture didn't work. In fact, Hennessey thought it rather comical, but more, it pointed to Golightly as a follower, someone who was easily led, and that, to Hennessey, suggested the man was innocent. In his experience, murders were always committed by the sort of person who thought the sun shone just for them, and that had always included the so-called 'crimes of passion'.

'I'll leave you with your client.' Hennessey stood. 'I'll return in a minute or two.'

'I'd appreciate that, thank you.' Croy nodded his thanks as Hennessey left the room.

Yellich, having set a nervous constable on an unpleasant errand, returned to the CID corridor and joined Hennessey beside the hot drinks vending machine.

'He's a bit pale,' Yellich said as he approached Hennessey. 'Young copper, first time he's broken bad news.'

'Well, we've all done it, it's one of the "first times" to remember, first time alone in uniform feeling everybody's eyes on you, first arrest, first "not guilty" plea to be contested. As I said, we've all done it. Tea? Coffee?'

'Tea, please, boss.'

Hennessey fed twenty-pence pieces into the machine and extracted the hot fluid in a white plastic beaker that he handed to the younger man. 'I'm half believing him.'

'Golightly? Thanks.'

'Yes.' Hennessey selected 'coffee no sugar' and pressed the button. 'I'm prepared to work very hard to get a conviction, but I also don't want to be diverted. The first few hours and all that...'

'Well, it's all there, skipper, means, motivation, skill ... he used to be a butcher...'

'Yes, I know.' Hennessey took the beaker of coffee from the machine. 'Ersatz,' he smiled.

'What?'

'Ersatz coffee, sort of coffee substitute the Germans drank during the Second World War. I'm sure the stuff from this machine lets us know what it tasted like. But yes, I am aware of that, but his attitude ... he's not over-egging it. You've seen television appeals when folk go in front of the camera urging their loved one to come home, and being in floods of tears as they do the urging, when all the while said loved one is in a shallow grave, having been laid there by the fair hand of the tearful urger.'

'Yes,' Yellich sipped his tea, 'excruciating to watch, but very useful ... dig holes for themselves, or folk see them on TV and phone and say, "He tried to kill me once."'

'Yes ... or tell us his name isn't Smith, it's Brown. As you say, very useful, but those people who sit in front of a press conference always over-egg it, they're just too tearful ... they are not Oscar-winning performances at all: too transparent, too emotional, especially in the UK, where we still value the stiff upper lip. I mean, compare their histrionics with the restrained dignity of genuinely bereaved people who make statements to the press after the conviction of the person who murdered their loved one.'

'Chalk and cheese.' Yellich sipped his tea.

'Yes. No similarity at all.' Hennessey pointed to the interview room. 'He is more like the second type. He is not the most pleasant man I have met.'

'You can say that again.'

'But he has a point. Some people row throughout their marriages, but in a strange way they are successful marriages.'

'It's not the sort of successful marriage I'd like.'

'Me neither, but he made the point that his parents had that sort of marriage. What was it he said? "My father wept at his wife's funeral." They'd been going at it like cat and dog for decades, and one wept at the other's funeral. He would have grown up witnessing that, and would have the propensity to ill temper, and if she had the same experiences, and they met...'

'Like finds like.' Yellich moved the beaker from one hand to the other. 'They find each other and recreate their parents' marriage. Yes, I see what you're saying, boss.'

'I'd still like to talk to her sister, see what insights she can offer about the state of the Golightly union.'

'Golightly...' Yellich smiled. 'Not a particularly apt surname.'

'It isn't really, is it?' Hennessey also allowed himself a brief smile. 'The other thing is that he showed concern for his brother and sister-in-law. In all my years on the force, I have never known a murderer to show such concern and consideration.'

'My years are less than yours, boss, but yes, that's not a trait you meet often in murderers. The murderers I have met have all been very self-orientated, even to the point of blaming the victim for their own murder. "She should have done what I told her to do, then I wouldn't have had to kill her." We have heard the like often, and will doubtless hear it again before we're finished.'

'Well, you certainly will, Yellich, you certainly will, but me,' Hennessey ran his liver-spotted hands through his grey hair, 'me, I can hear my pension calling my name.' It was with a sense of sadness that he dropped his beaker into the small wastebasket beside the vending machine. 'Well, round two.'

'Round two.' Yellich similarly dropped his beaker into the wastebasket.

'We'll keep our options open. We won't take our eyes off this rabbit just yet, but equally, we must keep an open mind.'

Hennessey, followed by Yellich, re-entered the interview room and re-took their seats.

Hennessey pressed the 'record' button and the twin cassettes began to rotate. Hennessey glanced at his watch and said, 'The time is twelve oh nine in the afternoon. The interview is resumed. I am DCI Hennessey, I am going to ask the other persons present to identify themselves.' When the formality of self-identification was complete, Hennessey asked, 'Why do you assume your wife went to stay with her sister on the occasions she left the house following an argument with you?'

'Because there's nowhere else she could go.'

'No friends?'

'If she had friends, I don't know of them.'

'You don't have children?'

'No, Mary can't. We tried to adopt, but the Social Work Department didn't approve. Had this social worker, a young woman in a woolly hat, visited a few times, and didn't we have one of our rows when she was there? Mary excelled herself, throwing the crockery ... the social worker was wide-eyed at that, don't think she'd seen anything like it. We were so preoccupied with arguing that neither of us noticed her leave the house. A day or two later, we got a letter thanking us for our interest in adopting but were deemed "inappropriate" candidates. So that was that. So, no children. Pity ... I ... well, never mind ... that was just the way of it in our marriage.'

'Were you faithful to your wife?'

'Chief Inspector!' Croy gasped. 'Where is the relevance of that?'

'The relevance of that question, sir, is that again, at this stage we do not know what is or is not relevant.' Hennessey's jaw set firm. He felt, he sensed, that he and Croy were developing a personal dislike of each other.

'I still protest the question.' He turned to Golightly and said, 'I advise you not to answer that.'

'I advise you to answer it.' Hennessey fixed Golightly with a cold stare. 'You see, Mr Golightly, there are, in fact, three answers to that question. You can answer "Yes", or you can answer "No", or you can refuse to answer, which in itself is a form of answer, and which is the most self-defeating because it allows us, the police, to place our own interpretation on your refusal to answer.'

'We'd wonder what you have to hide,' Yellich added. 'It tells us where to start digging.'

Golightly shrugged. 'Nothing to hide. I was faithful to Mary.'

Croy smiled smugly. 'Don't think you can go anywhere else, can you, Chief Inspector?'

'You are probably right,' Hennessey leaned back in his chair, 'for now.'

'For now?'

'For now.' Hennessey wore a stern expression as he folded his arms. 'Your client is still our prime suspect in the murder of Mrs Mary Golightly. We haven't the evidence to hold him and charge him with the offence.'

'So he is free to go?'

'He is. For now.'

The search of Golightly's house revealed a confused home, so thought Hennessey. Untidy, not necessarily unclean but very untidy, as though the Golightlys were happy to live in a mess because their lives, their marriage, were in a mess. Hennessey thought the state of the interior of the house suited the Golightlys as he was getting to know them. Or, at least, getting to know them as they had been. The lock-up, by interesting contrast, revealed itself to be neat and well-ordered. The lock-up contained the car, which was indeed a 'lovely old lady' of a beast, two-tone grey with white walled tyres, standing on blocks so as to lift the strain from the suspension. It sat sedately, it seemed to Hennessey, under a dustsheet, and, as if possessed of a human quality, seemed to him to be 'sniffing' indignantly at the sudden and most unwelcome intrusion into 'her' personal space. The tools in the lock-up clearly had a specific place of their own and the workbench at the rear was clean and tidy. The contrast between the interior of the house and the interior of the lock-up was large, and left Hennessey beginning to assume that the 'mess' was in the life of Mrs Golightly, probably compounded by some recent confusion on the part of Mr Golightly. But, if left to his own devices, Terence Golightly was fully in control of his environment and his life. His present dishevelled appearance, the unwashed dishes in the sink, the sudden concern for this brother and sister-in-law, all suddenly seemed to Hennessey to be a determined and convincing play to the gallery. His opinion of Golightly vacillated as the hours had elapsed, in the frame, out of the frame, back in the frame again, yet each time the man was in the frame, he seemed to be a little more appropriately placed, a little more snugly fitting than he was the last time he was there. But house or lock-up, neither showed signs of a struggle nor, to Hennessey, had the 'feel' of a crime scene.

'Where now, skipper?' Yellich asked as the constable secured the door of the lock-up, leaving the 'old lady' to resume her slumber, to be woken only when the classic car market picked up again.

'The sister, I think.' Hennessey accepted the key to the lock-up as it was proffered to him by the constable, with a nod of thanks. He held up the key. 'We'll drop this back to its rightful owner and go and pay a call.'

'She'll be distraught.' Yellich and Hennessey began to walk from the lock-up, crunching black grit under their feet as they fell into step with each other.

'Oh, we'll be very sensitive,' Hennessey replied, 'but her distress is likely to be useful. As you know, people tend to be less guarded when in that sort of emotional state.'

'She's not in the frame?' Yellich turned to Hennessey.

'Not as much as the husband of the victim, but at this moment Yellich, anybody and everybody is in the frame until we determine otherwise.'

It was Tuesday, 14.12 hours.

Three

Tuesday, 2 June, 15.00 hours – 22.30 hours
in which more is revealed about the Golightlys.

'You'll have to forgive me.' Mrs Ryan dabbed her eyes with a handkerchief, which was, by then, clearly saturated.

'It's all right.' Hennessey sitting opposite her spoke gently.

'Do you want me to go, Meryl?' The woman sitting beside Mrs Ryan seemed to Hennessey and Yellich to be genuinely concerned.

'No, no.' Mrs Ryan shook her head. 'Please stay.'

'I'm a neighbour.' The woman turned to Hennessey and Yellich. 'The constable who called earlier, he knocked on my door and asked me if I was friendly with Meryl. He said he'd brought bad news and asked if I was friendly with her, would I sit with her.

He didn't want to leave her alone.'

'I see.'

'Her husband can't be contacted, he's a lorry driver, long distance. He has a mobile phone but he keeps it switched off when he's in the cab.'

'Sensible.' Hennessey nodded. 'Responsible of him.' He read the room: neatly kept, signs of a steady income, a wide screen television, DVD player, coasters with 'Benidorm' and 'Ibiza' written on them, brightly-coloured furnishings, a print of Constable's *Haywain* on the wall above the fireplace, a compact music system on the sideboard. The room smelled heavily of air freshener. In its taste and decoration, it was monied Rawcliffe. The next-door property may well have a few scraps of carpet on otherwise bare floorboards and an ancient black and white television. That was also Rawcliffe.

'Maybe,' Mrs Ryan breathed deeply, 'but his job's on the line if the police catch him driving when he's talking on the mobile. He'll likely phone when he's at his rest stop, or he's offloaded. He's running a container down to Felixstowe today. When he phones,

I won't tell him about Mary, it'll take his mind off the road.' She again breathed deeply, collecting herself. 'So how can I help you gentlemen?'

'Well,' Hennessey began, 'I appreciate that this can't be easy for you.'

'You can say that again.' She forced a smile.

'Your sister, not just deceased, but murdered, and in such a way.' Hennessey paused. 'Sorry ... I must correct myself, we don't know how she was murdered. I meant that her body was treated in such a way.'

'Yes ... I know what you meant. It's all right.' Meryl Ryan smiled. 'Our Mary, who would want to harm her?'

'Which is why we are here. Do you know of anyone who would?'

Meryl Ryan shook her head. 'She had no enemies that we knew of. She wasn't a criminal ... you know how they bump each other off. We watch television, you see, so we know how criminals work.'

'I see.' Hennessey smiled, reflecting that he had been a policeman for all his working life and had yet to fully fathom the criminal

mind. If only he had known that all he had
to do was watch television, it would all have
been so much easier.

'So, nothing like that.'

'What was Mrs Golightly like as a person?'

'Mary? Quiet ... bookish. Never was the
life and soul of any party.'

'That's interesting.'

'Is it?'

'Yes, Mr Golightly ... he gave quite a different impression, as did their neighbours.
Both spoke of an argumentative house, rows
and walk-outs on Mrs Golightly's part.'

'Well, who wouldn't argue with that creep
she married? I mean, how could she have
brought that ... that ... thing into our family?
What could have possessed her? I knew it
would all turn sour, but not this sour.'

'Why do you say he's a "creep"?'

'Well, he's a serial infidel, isn't he?'

'A serial what?'

'Infidel ... someone who commits infidelity. That's an infidel, isn't it?'

'I don't think that's quite what the word
means, but I understand. Mr Golightly
wasn't a faithful husband?'

'You can say that again.'

'That's interesting. He claimed not to have had extra-marital lovers.'

'Ha! Well, he would, wouldn't he? The number of times Mary's come here in floods of tears because he's taunted her with his latest playing away from home ... but she always went back to him. It's so hurtful ... I remember her as a little girl ... she was my little sister. I remember her, as you would, she was such a happy mite, and then her marriage to the butcher. How such a lovely little girl should end up having her life ruined by that rat? It carries such a long way.'

'What?'

'A bad marriage. Even if you get divorced, the contamination is still there. I mean, I'm lucky.'

'So am I,' the lady neighbour offered.

'Yes, we've both been lucky with our men. We made a good choice. All right, they're working-class, but then so are we, we came off the estate here, we knew each other from school, me and Liz here.'

The neighbour, evidently Liz, beamed at

Hennessey.

'Aye, I knew little Mary too,' Liz added.

'Well, our husbands aren't frightened of work.'

'My Stuart's a taxi-driver,' Liz said proudly.

'See, they both bring home the bacon and they don't play away from home. My husband stays out overnight because he hasn't the time to return, and he gets drunk with other lorry drivers and watches porno films with them, but that's all right, he doesn't play away from home and that's the main thing. But Terry Golightly ... he was well named, Golightly from bed to bed to bed.'

'It is a good name for him,' Liz nodded. 'A very good name. Never thought of it like that before.'

'You wouldn't know of any of his ... his...'

'Bits on the side, you mean?' Again there was clear anger in Meryl Ryan's voice.

'About half the women in York,' Liz said. 'About half.'

'You can say that again.' Meryl Ryan thumped the arm of the chair in which she sat. 'About half. I told you he was a serial infidel, even if that's not the right word. But he was a serial something.'

'Something you tread on in the street,' offered Liz.

'You can say that again. That about sums the creep up.' Meryl Ryan's jaw set hard. 'That's it. Terry Golightly is something you scrape off the sole of your shoe.'

'Any names you know of?'

'Names?'

'Of Mr Golightly's girlfriends?'

'I don't know any names, do you, Liz?'

'Don't know names.'

'Where would a man of his age go to meet partners? Do you know that?'

'Nightclubs?' Meryl Ryan glanced at Liz, her neighbour. 'I think he went to those.'

'Yes ... in York or in Leeds or Sheffield.'

'He put himself about a little?' Hennessey said.

'A little, yes, you could say that.' Meryl Ryan shook her head. 'Yes, a little, that's one way of putting it.'

'He didn't strike me as the nightclubbing type.'

'Well, that's because you only saw Terence

Golightly the slob. There's another Terence Golightly, Terence Golightly the dandy, the man about town. Smartly dressed, clean-shaven, flashing money about ... that's the Terence Golightly who goes out at night looking for action in the nightclubs while his wife is at home doing the ironing.'

'Did your sister suspect him of infidelity?'

'Didn't have to, he boasted of it, so she said.'

'Yet they stayed married?'

'She was beginning divorce proceedings. So she said.'

'Interesting.' Hennessey sat back in the chair. 'Did Mr Golightly know about that?'

'I think so.' Meryl Ryan held eye contact with Hennessey. 'She told me that she had told him.'

Hennessey and Yellich glanced at each other.

'Why?' Meryl Ryan asked with a sense of urgency, noticing the look exchanged between the two officers. 'Is that important?'

'Well, it's just that Mr Golightly's version is not the same as yours. We can't say too much, you understand, but he claims to have been faithful to Mrs Golightly.'

'Ha!' Liz snorted. Mrs Ryan gasped.

'He also claims the marriage was sound, despite the arguments.'

'Would you believe it?' Meryl Ryan and Liz looked at each other. 'Well, I can tell you he's lying through his teeth.'

'Seems he may be.' Hennessey spoke softly. He thought the two women to be genuine, more genuine than he had found Mr Terence Golightly to be.

'Well, don't take our word for it.'

'No?'

'No, ask Mr Thornton, her solicitor.'

Yellich delved into his pocket and retrieved his notebook. 'Thornton, you say?'

'Yes. Don't know the address but he's with Innes and Co, in York.'

'Innes and Co?'

'She told me his name a few times and we have a family friend by that name. No connection, but it helps me remember his name. Anyway, he'll tell you whether or not she was seeking a divorce. And you might ask him what happened to his first wife.'

There was a stunned silence which lasted

five or six seconds and was broken by Hennessey, who said, 'First wife?'

'First wife,' Meryl Ryan nodded, allowing herself a knowing look and a brief smile.

'Tell me about her.'

'She was the cause of the first argument, not long after they were married. She, Mary I mean, never knew about number one wife, not until number one son appeared at their door one day. Just turned up out of the blue looking for his father. It was then, and only then, that my sister learned that she was number two wife. That didn't go down too well.'

'I can imagine. What do you know about "number one wife", as you call her?'

'Those were Mary's words actually ... she was in floods when she told me, "I'm number two wife," she said, "second chance, that's me." Anyway, she disappeared.'

'Oh, no.' Hennessey sighed as the implication struck him.

'Oh, yes.' Again Meryl Ryan smiled. 'Rings bells. Heard it before somewhere? They had two children, very young children, when number one wife disappeared. They were fostered, for some reason. Anyway, then the eldest son turned up out of the blue wanting to meet his real father, they went to the village for a drink in the pub, leaving Mary feeling devastated. That's the sort of man he is, insensitive, secretive, and a liar.'

'Do you know where we can trace the son?'

'Easy to find, same name as his dad, Terence Golightly, came knocking on my sister's door when he got released from prison. So you'll know him. He'll be about twenty-two ... twenty-three by now.'

'Probably back inside,' Liz snorted.

'That's probably true,' Meryl Ryan nodded. 'My sister said he was a "shifty" looking character. She used that word, "shifty".'

'This has been very interesting.' Hennessey looked at Meryl Ryan and then at her neighbour. 'Very interesting indeed.' He paused. 'Do you know of anything else that might help us?'

'Can't think of anything.'

Hennessey stood, and Yellich did likewise. Hennessey handed Mrs Ryan his card. 'If you do remember anything, anything at all, please contact us.'

'I will.' Mrs Ryan took the card, read it, and placed it on her mantelpiece. 'I hope you nail him. He ruined my sister's life, and now he's gone and murdered her.'

'We'll do all we can, for the sake of justice.'

Returning from Rawcliffe, along Clifton Road, towards Micklegate Bar, Hennessey said, 'So what have we got?'

'A very contradictory muddle, skipper,' Yellich replied, keeping his eyes on the road, both hands on the wheel. 'Well, we've got Golightly's story – full of holes.'

'Yes, he'll have to be re-interviewed, but I don't want to go rushing at him. Before we see him again, we'll do our homework. We were ill-prepared this morning, that's probably my fault. We'll go and chat to Mrs Golightly's colleagues at the health centre. I'll do that. Can you ask Criminal Records what they have on Terence Golightly Junior? Important to be prepared, Yellich. Very important.'

'Yes, sir,' Yellich responded dryly. He didn't know to whom Hennessey was speaking, whether Hennessey was speaking to him or to himself. Yellich felt Hennessey blaming himself for being a little ill prepared ... but Yellich didn't need to comment, and he felt a wall begin to develop between them.

'If he's local, go and see him.' Hennessey paused, as Yellich turned right into Water End. 'What did that young fella you interviewed tell you about the car he heard in the road ... big and expensive, wasn't it?'

'Yes, boss.'

'What sort of car does Golightly Senior drive?'

'Don't know, boss.'

'I'll check that one out when I visit the health centre.' He glanced at his watch, 'Four fifteen p.m. If you can't get hold of Golightly Junior easily, leave it until tomorrow.'

'Thanks, boss, Sara will be relieved. The summer is difficult for her, with Jeremy being like he is, poor lad, lovely lad ... but he can be difficult. I'd like to get there as soon as.'

'OK,' said Hennessey. 'Just find out where

he is and pick it up tomorrow. I'll go to the health centre anyway, catch them when they're closing.'

Hennessey got out of Yellich's car in the car park at the rear of Micklegate Bar Police Station and walked across the concrete to where he had parked his own car, and unlocked it. He was met by a blast of hot air, and wound the windows down and left the car door open for a minute before sitting behind the steering wheel. He did not like motor vehicles at the best of times, and any inconvenience, like an oven-hot car, or a traffic jam, would irritate him more than it would any other motorist. Eventually, he deemed the air within his car to be breathable and drove out of York to Gravely and to the health centre, which he found situated on Summer Pasture Lane. He found the name of the road to be delightful and approached the door with an uplifted heart.

'Do you have an appointment?' The lady behind the reception desk smiled the question. She was in her late middle years and wore a floral-patterned lightweight dress. A watch on her wrist and two rings on her wedding finger were her only decoration.

'No.' Hennessey returned the smile. Unlike Mrs Ryan's house of earlier that day, the smell of air freshener in the surgery was not overwhelming, but more delicate, more in the background, he thought, more a fragrance, more of a scent than an odour. 'Sorry.'

'Ah ... we can really only see people with an appointment, you see. I could see if one of the doctors is free, but I think we are booked up.'

'It's all right.' Hennessey showed his ID. 'It's not that sort of help I need.'

'Oh ... it'll be about Mary?'

'It will.'

'Terrible business.' She looked down. 'Really terrible. We really can't believe it.'

'It takes time.' Hennessey glanced about him. The interior of the health centre was decorated with pastel shades; there was much clear, natural light coming into the building through plentiful glass, and a calendar behind the reception desk, opened at June, showed a green steam locomotive and passenger vehicles crossing the Ribblehead Viaduct. 'Did you know her?'

'Yes. Quite well. We worked together for this last year.' She turned. 'That's her desk, over there.' She raised an arm towards a solid-looking desk, with a neatly-kept working surface, and on which sat a word processor.

'Do you mind if I take a look in the drawers?'

'I'll really need to ask the practice manager.' She picked up the phone and dialled a two-figure internal number.

'How many people work here?' Hennessey asked while the receptionist waited for her call to be answered.

'Well, two doctors, Dr Maudsley and Dr Fryer, a practice nurse, Nurse Lee, the practice manager...' she lifted the phone away from her cheek, 'Mr Ringrose, and me, I'm Mrs March.'

'Mrs March...?'

'Wasn't so bad when I was growing up ... I was June Turner, then I got wed and became June March.' She smiled. 'He must be out of his office ... oh ... hello, Mr Ring-rose. Can you come to reception, please? There's a police officer here, asking about Mary. He wants to look in Mary's desk ... Yes ... yes, all right. Thank you.' She replaced the handset. 'Mr Ringrose says by all means you can look in Mary's desk. Would you like to come round, down the side here?'

Hennessey walked down a small corridor at the side of the reception desk, turned left at the end and entered the reception area.

'Oh, and there's a blood nurse.'

'A blood nurse?'

'Comes in for a clinic once a week to take blood samples from patients. It's usually a different nurse each time, usually, but for the last three weeks the Area Health Authority has sent the same nurse.'

'I see. This is Mrs Golightly's desk?'

'Yes.'

Hennessey sat in the chair that squeaked as he did so. 'Did Mrs Golightly only use the desk?'

'Well, sometimes she stood at the count-er...'

Hennessey smiled. 'Point to you. My command of syntax isn't what it should be. I meant, did only Mrs Golightly use this desk?'

'Oh...' Mrs March laughed nervously. 'Yes. Nobody else used it.'

'The drawers are locked.' Hennessey tried the drawers, three, on the right-hand side.

'Oh ... yes, practice rules. Mr Ringrose is very strict about that.'

'Mr Ringrose is very strict about what?' The voice belonged to a smartly-dressed man in his thirties. He smiled as he spoke.

'About locking up, Mr Ringrose,' June March explained.

'Quite right.' The voice belonged to a similarly smartly-dressed man with a stethoscope around his neck, who walked round a corner and into the reception area. 'Sorry, but I couldn't help overhearing.'

'Dr Maudsley.' Ringrose turned and smiled: he was clearly pleased to have support.

'Well, patients to see.' He walked to the waiting room. Hennessey returned the smile and wondered if he had seen Maudsley before ... he felt he had, but couldn't place him.

'Yes, I am strict about locking up. We have drugs on the practice, and confidential files, all of which have to be kept securely locked up. My view is that if you are in the habit of locking everything that can be locked, then you're certain to lock the things that have to be locked. It's when you get into the practice of not locking the unimportant locks that the important locks will eventually, one day, be left unlocked. So keep it tight.'

'Good idea.'

'Well it has worked so far. Every lock is locked at the close of the day. We are all in the habit of locking every lock.'

'We go on automatic pilot when we're closing up.' Mrs March smiled. 'Lock all locks.'

'Well ... how can I get into this desk, or rather the drawers of the same?'

'I keep a spare key in my office. I'll be back in a mo...' Ringrose turned and walked away.

'He's very efficient,' offered Mrs March.

'Oh, yes...' Hennessey smiled. 'I can see

that.' He glanced round the reception area. Then he asked, 'Did you know Mrs Golightly well enough to know about her private life?'

'Well, it's not for me to gossip.'

'It's not gossip, Mrs March. It's helping the police with a murder investigation.'

'If you put it like that ... and it's the investigation into someone I regarded as a friend.'

'Well, I do put it like that ... and if she was a friend of yours...'

A lady walked up to the reception desk and said she had an appointment with Dr Maudsley.

'Mrs Reid?' asked Mrs March, consulting the appointment book.

'Yes.'

'If you'd like to go and take a seat in the waiting room.' Mrs March then turned and addressed Hennessey. 'See what you find in her desk first ... but I can't talk here, and I probably don't have anything of interest to say.'

'Well, you let me be the judge of that.'

'I live just round the corner.' She glanced

up at the clock on the wall. 'That lady was the last appointment of the day. When she leaves, I can lock up. The doctors and Mr Ringrose let themselves out, the nurse has gone on visits and won't be back until tomorrow. I live on Priory Rise.'

'Priory Rise?'

'Number fourteen.'

'Fourteen?'

'Left out of the door, first left off Summer Meadow Lane, that's Priory Rise. Can't miss my house ... it's the one with the windmill in the front garden.'

'The windmill.' He smiled. 'Doubt if I'll miss that. Thank you.'

Ringrose strode confidently up to the desk and handed Mrs March a key on a yellow key fob. 'If you'll hand this to the officer, please.' Hennessey took the key and read the fob legend. It read 'Reception – Desk Two'. Very efficient, he thought.

Hennessey inserted the key into the lock on the inside of the desk. He found it to be, like the working surface, very neatly kept. It was, he felt, the very sort of desk that was kept in a way that would appeal to Chief

Superintendent Sharkey: everything in its proper place. Hennessey was the first to admit that he was no clinical psychologist, but here, in front of him, was not the desk he had anticipated. The picture that had thus far emerged of Mrs Mary Golightly was of a woman whose life was in turmoil. Her marriage was violent, certainly verbally so if not physically. She was beginning divorce proceedings, and consequently, Hennessey expected to find chaos within the drawers, confusion, a mess, disorder. Instead he found the opposite: neatness, good order, logic, common sense in the arrangement of the items in the desk. Mary Golightly was a woman on top of her life. That observation just did not tally with the impression he had been given of her. It certainly didn't tally with the confusion that was the interior of her house.

He began to explore the desk. The neatly-kept drawers aside, he was not surprised by their contents. He found only what he would expect to find in a drawer in a desk in the reception area of a health centre. He found items of stationery, he found a pocket medical dictionary, well thumbed, as if Mrs Golightly, when typing a doctor's letter, might have to type the name of a medical condition which would prompt her to think, 'What on earth is that?' and then consult the dictionary which she had bought. There was a conventional dictionary, the Concise Oxford, also well thumbed, a bottle of aspirin, a needle and thread, spare print paper, a pair of spectacles in a reinforced case. There was nothing as useful as a diary or a wedge of poison pen letters. Hennessey slid the drawers shut and glanced up as the elderly patient, Mrs Reid, walked past the reception desk towards the exit. Hers had clearly been a very quick consultation.

'Well, I can secure the reception area and go home now. That's the last patient of the day. She's a heartsink.'

'Really?'

'Yes. Very good condition for her age, just needs a lot of reassuring that all is well. Comes in once a fortnight. The doctors know her well and that we ... well, me now, ask that I give her the last appointment of the day. Helps them wind down.'

'I see.'

'So ... find anything? Not my place to ask, I know.'

'No, I didn't. But your co-operation is appreciated.'

Dr Maudsley reappeared at the reception desk. 'Just checking that that's it.'

'Yes, doctor.' June March smiled, though her tone was deferential. 'Just one "no show" today. Mrs O'Brien had the two p.m., she didn't come in.'

'She's done that before.' The doctor had close-cut ginger hair, about late forties, Hennessey thought, with the sort of chiselled features that women would find appealing. He had a kind of classic attractiveness that made Hennessy feel that he'd seen him before – as he had, almost, on the covers of men's magazines, on posters in shop windows, presenting the face of traditional good looks. 'I'll talk to her about that next time she comes in.'

'She didn't do any harm today, doctor, we had vacant appointments.'

'Still ... if she does that in the middle of a flu epidemic, she does someone out of a consultation which could be lifesaving.' He glanced up at Hennessey. 'Hello again. Is there any news about Mary?'

'Not yet,' Hennessy told him.

'Dreadful business.' Maudsley raised his eyebrows. 'You read such things but you never think it would happen to someone you know.'

'Yes...' Hennessey said. 'As you say, you hear of such things, read of them, but it's always someone else's tragedy. Then one day...'

'You sound as though you speak from experience, Mr Hennessey.'

Hennessey paused. He felt a sudden urge to give of himself to Dr Maudsley, but checked the urge. 'No ... just a cop for too long, broken bad news to too many people.'

'I see.' Maudsley tapped the surface of the reception counter. 'Well, if we can be of assistance...'

'Mrs March and Mr Ringrose have been fully cooperative. Thank you.'

'Good. Good.' Maudsley turned and walked back to his consulting room.

'I'd rather not be seen leaving with you,

Mr Hennessey.' June March turned to Hennessey.

'I understand.' Hennessey smiled. 'I'll leave now. The house with the windmill in the front garden?'

'Yes ... well, cottage really.'

'A cottage with a windmill in the front garden. That sounds even more intriguing.' He smiled again and walked out of the health centre.

The windmill was two feet high and surrounded by ornamental gnomes. Hennessey waited without having to muster patience, because Priory Rise he found to be a delightful enclave of prosperous-looking cottages with neatly-tended gardens. A man digging his garden in the adjacent cottage, wearing a blue shirt, a sunhat and corduroy trousers smiled at him and mouthed, 'Good afternoon.'

'Afternoon,' Hennessey called back with just sufficient volume to allow his voice to carry. There was a tranquillity about Priory Rise which he didn't want to violate. A woman turned into the drive atop a magnificent-looking horse, a black mare with a glistening coat which had a steady, measured tread, clip, clip, clip, clip; the woman too smiled warmly at Hennessey and bade him 'Good afternoon.' A pleasant change from most horse riders who, in Hennessey's experience, tended to give the impression that they were not just looking down at foot passengers, but looking down their noses at them. But this horsewoman was different, and induced Hennessey to doff his Panama in reply. He felt he could be well content to live in Priory Rise.

June March appeared, bumbling up the road, clearly anxious not to keep Hennessey waiting, for she seemed to Hennessey to be walking too rapidly in the heat to be comfortable. 'Sorry, sorry,' she panted as she approached him.

'There was someone in her life and it wasn't her husband.' June March spoke quietly, then brushed past Hennessey, reached for a key in her pocket and opened the front door of her cottage, all in one flowing movement. She entered the house. 'Come in,' she called, 'come in, come in.'

The interior of the cottage was cool. In

terms of proportion, Hennessey found it too cramped for his taste, but there was no escaping the fact that it was cosy, very cosy indeed. The building gave him the feeling that it would keep its occupants safe and warm and dry in any storm or tempest.

'Would you like a cup of tea? I'm going to have one.' June March dropped her handbag in a chair and hurried towards the rear of the house, presumably, thought Hennessey, to the kitchen.

'Yes,' he called after her, 'if you are making one. Thank you ... that would be very nice.' He cast his eyes around the room. Mrs March's taste in home decoration wasn't his. His taste did not extend to placing little household gnomes around the room to complement the gnomes in the garden. Nor did he like artificial flowers and fruit and models of furry animals.

'Take a seat, take a seat.' Mrs March bustled back into the room, holding a tray of tea for two.

'So, she had someone in her life?' asked Hennessey when moments later he was sipping a refreshing cup of tea.

'Yes. Just lately. She always looked so happy, so content, so fulfilled. Yet she always complained about her husband. Only one explanation there.'

'Do you know who the man was?'

'No. She was very discreet. I couldn't tell you this at the health centre, someone might have heard.'

'I understand. That's all right.'

'Thank you. Well, I don't know who it was, to be truthful.'

'Any ideas?'

'Not the slightest.'

'All right. How long had the affair been going on?'

'Not long.' June March stirred her tea. 'It was still in the new stage. One day she just wasn't the same any more.'

'The same?'

'Well, normally Mary looked troubled, browbeaten, preoccupied, worried, a lot on her mind. She was a woman with a troubled marriage. It all seemed to fit. Then a few weeks ago she seemed a new woman, she seemed uplifted, she had a glow about her, she looked bonny.'

'Bonny?'

'It's the only word I can think of. It just suited her, attractive, with a warmth; not like those stick insects you see modelling swimsuits, their beauty has a coldness about it, but Mary just looked good and gave the impression that if you put your hands up to her they'd get warm.'

'Yes, I know what you mean. About how long ago did she start looking "bonny"?'

'Not too long ago.'

'Well weeks? Months?'

'Days, I'd say. Possibly a week.'

'That recent?'

'Yes. Like I said, they were very new to each other.'

'This is interesting. He didn't phone her at work or anything?'

'Not to my knowledge.'

'So you never heard a first name, or a pet name?'

'No, nothing like that at all. As I said, she was discreet.'

'Is there anything you can tell me about him? Any impression you gleaned?'

'He seemed to have money. She suddenly

started to wear bracelets and a new watch, an expensive-looking watch.'

'Did she arrive and leave with them on?'

'Yes, but she could easily have hidden them from her husband, if she wanted to. Because she arrived at work with them and left with them on doesn't mean to say that she left home wearing them and arrived home wearing them.'

'No ... agreed, but equally, she could have taunted her husband with them. Sorry...' Hennessey paused. 'Just thinking aloud.'

'Is this helpful?'

'Yes, very. It adds a very big piece to the jigsaw puzzle that we are putting together of Mary Golightly's life. A very large and significant piece indeed. How long had she worked at the health centre?'

'About a year. I've been there longest. There's been a complete staff change in that time, two new doctors, a new practice manager, new nurse, and Mary ... all in twelve months. We're still getting to know each other really. The original doctors both retired, so we got Dr Maudsley, he's very nice, and Dr Fryer, she's a bit of a cold fish

I think, but she has won the respect of many of the patients. Mr Ringrose arrived shortly after Mary. His predecessor moved to a larger practice, more money. Then the new nurse joined us. It's all been a hurly-burly of a time, and very recently Mary stopped looking morose and started looking bonny. And then...' June March looked at the carpet. 'It's still not fully sunk in.'

'It'll take time.'

'I imagine you have seen all this before?'

'Yes, I have.' Hennessey put his empty cup on the tray which June March had set on a low table. 'It's all part of the job.' He stood. 'Well, thank you, Mrs March. It has been very useful, very useful indeed. If you think of anything else that you feel may be of interest, please let us know.' He took his card from his wallet and handed it to her. 'I can be reached at that number.'

'Micklegate Bar,' Mrs March read the card. 'I haven't been in York for a long time. Micklegate Bar? That's the gate near the railway station, isn't it?'

'Well, yes, leave the station, turn right and that's the gate you come to.'

'That's where Harry Hotspur's head was left impaled for three years, if I remember my school history.'

'Not just Harry Hotspur,' Hennessey smiled, 'but many others as well, other traitors, rebels and enemies of the Crown.'

'Difficult times...'

Hennessey sensed a sudden desperation in Mrs March, as if she yearned for him to stay and was disappointed that he was taking his leave. 'Well I imagine Mr March will be coming home soon?'

'Sadly, he won't. He passed over last year.'

'I'm sorry.'

'It's the way of it. He wasn't old, not young, but not old either. That's life. It has no rhyme or reason. It's just the way of it.'

Hennessey drove directly home from Gravely. He wanted to avoid the main roads, which he knew would be heavy with homebound traffic at that hour. He drove down rural lanes, stopping occasionally to consult the road atlas that he kept open at the relevant page, drove through quiet villages with quaint, ancient names, and he found the villages and their names uplifted his spirits as he encountered them in flat countryside under a sun that was still high in the sky: Elvington, Kexby, High Catten, Stamford Bridge, Sand Hutton, Claxton, West Lilling, Sheriff Hutton, Farlington, Stillington ... until finally he arrived at Easingwold. He joined the Thirsk Road when he had negotiated the centre of the small town he was driving through, and his heart leapt as he saw a silver BMW parked half on, half off the grass verge. He signalled to make a right turn, and drove into the driveway of a solid-looking detached house. He left his car and heard his dog barking excitedly from within. Hennessey let himself in the front door and walked down the hallway and shook hands with the owner of the silver BMW. Later, the two men sat on the patio drinking tea from mugs whilst Oscar kept himself contentedly in the shade. He was a brown dog, and like all dark dogs, he suffered dreadfully in the heat.

'I'm in Middlesborough all this week.' Charles Hennessey sipped his tea, as he looked out across the rear garden where shadows were just beginning to lengthen, and over which swallows dived and circled to catch flying insects.

'Oh, yes?'

'Yes, he's going N.G., and this time I really believe it.'

'Oh?'

'He is charged with murder, a middle-aged lady, but there is hardly any evidence to support the charge that I can see. He knew her, he doesn't deny that, and he was seen close to where her body was found at the time of the death, so far as said time of death can be fixed.'

'Yes...' Hennessey smiled. 'Our pathologist, very good at her job, lovely lady as well, she avoids being drawn on that question. So difficult to pin down the time of death scientifically, she says. Once she said, if you accept the person died some time between when he or she was last seen alive by a reliable witness, and when the body was found, then that is as close as science could also get.'

'Interesting. I might use that. The prosecution are fielding a pathologist. He'll be in the witness box tomorrow, time of death being crucial to their case. Thanks, that observation will be very useful. Anyway, he has no motive for killing her and the place where the body was found was a public park. He had every right to be there.'

'Of course.'

'It's not as though her body was found in a derelict building from which he was seen emerging and running away. If that was the case then he might have some explaining to do ... but it's not. She was found behind a large rhododendron bush and he was seen walking along the pathway on the other side of the bush.'

'No DNA?'

'No, no trace evidence can be linked to him.'

'How was she murdered?'

'Blunt object to the head. There would have been blood spatter, quite widespread, but he hadn't a trace of it on his clothing. It really is a puzzle why the police put him in the frame in the first place. It's going to take a perverse jury to convict him on the strength of their case, but that's been known to happen.'

'Sadly, both ways as well. Perverse judgements have freed felons who were clearly guilty.'

'Indeed. Anyway, I have told him he can view the trial with confidence, but we are not out of the woods until the foreperson of the jury stands up and says, "Not guilty". If he or she says "Guilty", we'll lodge an immediate appeal, so he mustn't lose hope, even then.'

'Well, good luck.'

'Thanks. So what are you up to?'

'The leg in the bag inquiry.'

'Oh, that's landed on your lap?'

'For my sins, yes.'

'I read about it. Where's the rest of her?'

'In a body of water somewhere. There was a brick in the bag. Dr D'Acre, our pathologist, that's the lady who won't be drawn on the time of death, she pointed out that the stone could only be there to ensure it sank.'

'Sounds logical.'

'Yes, I wouldn't argue, but it begs the question why he didn't put the leg with, as you say, the rest of her.'

'Anybody in the frame?'

'Her husband is the only likely candidate, we've got more on him than the Teeside police sound to have on the man you're defending, but it's still not enough. Yet. He had a previous wife who disappeared, apparently.'

'Oh?'

'Yes, that's what my sergeant and I thought.'

'Well, I wish you well. I'm sure you'll get there. So, how are my bears?'

'Growing by the hour, it seems. Want to know when their granddad is coming to visit them again.'

'When I can, you couldn't keep me away. Grandchildren are much more fun.'

'Yes ... it couldn't have been easy for you, Dad, by yourself.'

'I had help.'

'A daily woman to come and clean. I know she did more than that but she was never a partner ... not like I have. I couldn't do it alone, not without Diane.'

Charles Hennessey paused. 'And we want to know when you are going to introduce us to your lady?'

'Oh ... soon. I'm sure you'll like her. I am certain Jennifer approves.'

'Approves? You mean, would approve?'

Hennessey smiled. 'Yes, I mean would approve, of course, I mean would approve.'

Four

Wednesday, 3 June,
10.20 hours – 13.35 hours
*in which Hennessey makes a useful trip to
Harrogate and later pays a call on a sugar baby.*

Yellich thought him a con's con. He also thought him a cop's con. He had ginger hair, close-cropped; icy-cold, green, piercing eyes. The sleeves of his blue cotton shirt were rolled up cuff-over-cuff, military style, revealing muscular forearms heavily and clumsily self-tattooed. He was a man who knew how to survive in the slammer, who knew the unwritten rules, who respected the convicts' code. He was the sort of man, Yellich realized, who knew his place in the scheme of things, who wouldn't look for trouble, but who could handle himself if trouble came calling. He was a man who would enjoy respect and personal space. A con's con. He was also a man who knew the futility of fighting when the game was up, who wouldn't resist arrest if caught red-handed, who wouldn't struggle on the hook like a salmon, but would give up like a carp or a pike and would confess to what he knew could be proven, but only to what he knew could be proven. A cop's con. His numbers put his age at twenty-two, nudging twenty-three.

'You look relieved.' Yellich pushed the packet of cigarettes across the table. He held up his lighter and pressed the ignition. The flame was large and instant.

'I am.' Terence Golightly junior drew heavily on the cigarette. 'My ounce is gone. An ounce of tobacco a week, what good is that? On the outside I can go through an ounce a day. I have a tobacco baron, little guy, gives me his ounce in return for protection, and he gets it. I put a guy in the hospital wing for causing my baron grief. So that's two days I get, two days every seven days. Five days of agony.'

Yellich took the packet of cigarettes and

pocketed them. 'Well, I can't let you have these, they'll be contraband. It could cost me my job. But I do have this, if you can be discreet.' He pulled an ounce of Dutch rolling tobacco in a blue pouch out of his pocket, together with a book of Rizla skins.

Terence Golightly gasped as he saw it, his eyes bulged: a hungry man looking at food, a thirsty man looking at clean, ice-cool drinking water. 'I can be discreet, sir. For that I can be very discreet. Especially since you're not after me for something.'

'You have something to hide?'

'Of course. We all have. That's the way it works, you do a few missions, maybe eight, nine missions, have success, then you get captured for the tenth mission. So, yeah, I done missions you know about, but you don't know I done them. Same with every con in here, except the ones like my baron, never done a thing wrong in his life, not even a parking ticket, then he goes and murders his wife, goes down for life. He's been in for five years now and he's still walking round like it's his first day at school.'

'You haven't been in here for five years?'

'Me? No. I was transferred from youth custody.'

'Five years for distributing cocaine.'

'Yes. I'll be out in three. Another year and a bit.'

'What are you going to do?'

'Cover my tracks better.' Golightly grinned.

'Not going straight?'

'Me? No ... my path is set; I'm a career blagger. I'm going to be bouncing in and out for the rest of my days. See, once you're on this side of the fence, you can't change to the other, it's not easy, not as easy as those female magistrates think it is. Your mates are on this side of the fence, the way you think is on this side of the fence, the thrills are on this side of the fence, the money is on this side of the fence. Most drug-smuggling missions are successful. If they weren't, there wouldn't be so many smack-heads on the street, sleeping rough and mugging elderly people or children for a few quid here and there.'

'Doesn't that bother you?'

'The smack-heads?' Golightly glanced up at the opaque pane of glass, which was set high in the cream-painted agent's room. 'No. Why should it? The demand is there. If we didn't supply it, somebody else would.'

Yellich remained silent. He had heard that argument, that rationalization, so many times before. You can't argue with a closed mind, he had once been told, so don't try.

'Anyway, the word is, things are going to get easier for you in future.'

'Oh, yes? How's that?'

'Well, the clever organizations are moving into people-smuggling. Just as much dosh to be had, but the sentences are less, which means the cowboys are taking over the drug-smuggling. You'll have a lot more success with the cowboys than with the team I'm in. I work for the man.'

'Who's he?'

Golightly grinned and tapped the side of his nose. 'This is my apprenticeship. You don't move up in the organization until you've got prison time under your belt. So I'm happy. I'm coming out to a good future.'

'Dare say we'll be seeing each other again.'

'Not if I can help it.'

'So, tell me about your father.'

'The butcher,' Golightly sneered. 'Don't know whether to thank him or hate him. It's through him I'm here. He just let me run wild and fed me when I came home, so, of course, I got into trouble with the law. But then I'm with the firm, so I'm moving up, going further. People-smuggling, that's big business. I've already got money put aside.'

'That can be taken from you.'

'Asset seizure, if I can't prove it's lawful, it's taken from me.'

'Yes.'

'Aye, but you've got to find it first.'

'Where is it? A Swiss bank?'

'No, in a building society.' Golightly paused. 'Not in my name, though.'

'How did you manage that?'

'Created a false identity.'

'That's not easy.'

'It's easy enough. Real birth certificate of someone your age who has died. I happened to know someone who was killed when he was seventeen. I knew his date of birth ...

went to the Registry Office...'

'In York?'

'No.' Golightly smiled. 'Do you think I'd be telling you this if it was close to home? You could work out my false ID then. No, it was another town and well out of Yorkshire. Walked in and asked for a copy of "my" birth certificate, paid a few quid and walked out with it. Used it to get a passport, forged the witness signature on the passport, gave my occupation as "teacher". Got the passport with no trouble at all. So I am beginning to build up a new ID. Opened a Post Office savings account and started paying money in. Then opened a building society account. I had an address, a passport, a good record with the Post Office. Showed them my passbook, just needed a reference then. Well, the boss wrote one for me, so I opened an account in my dead mate's name. Pay in hard cash regularly. I go in in working clothes and pay the money in, like I'm working for cash in hand. So they can have what Terence Golightly has in his name, but they can't link me to John Brown's money. John Brown's not the name

I use.' He drew hard on the nail.

'Of course,' Yellich smiled. 'Clever.' Then he thought, If only it was that easy. It's only a matter of time before the Inland Revenue catches up with you and finds out that 'John Brown' hasn't had a National Insurance number. He needed Golightly's co-operation, though, so he remained quiet.

'So your father let you run wild? We understand your mother disappeared.'

A pained look crossed Golightly's icy eyes. 'He killed her.'

'Tell me about it.'

'Well,' Golightly drew on the cigarette, 'no proof, didn't see anything...'

Yellich sat back in his chair. 'OK, in your own time, anything goes ... anything you suspect.'

'Well.' Golightly also sat back in his chair. 'That's just it, see, only what I suspect, the police were not interested. Took a statement and that was it, so far as I recall. I wasn't very old then, just a kid, about four, five. After that I got brought up by my dad's girl-friends, when he had one. There were long periods when it was just me and him in the house. But I knew all along. I just knew he'd murdered her. He took me to his butcher's shop, when he had one, and I watched him slice up a carcass, a cow, just carved it up so effortlessly, just took it apart, really sharp knife, and knowing where to cut, and a hacksaw for the bones, in a matter of minutes it was in pieces, ready to be put in the window. Just watching him, I knew he'd done that to my mum.'

'OK. You know your father, you know his haunts.'

'Haunts?'

'Where he goes.'

'Oh ... nothing to do with haunting then, like a ghost?'

'Not really.' Yellich grinned. 'Where would your father be likely to have put your mother's body?'

'He's cunning. My dad is smart. He's a real slob, the way he dresses ... but don't be fooled by that. He's playing games, he wants you to think he's sloppy,' Golightly tapped the side of his head, 'but he has more up here than you'd give him credit for. So nowhere he's likely to go. Won't be in the house.'

'Or his lock-up?'

'No.' Golightly fell silent and again drew deeply on the cigarette.

'What was your father like ... on a day to day basis?' Yellich pressed.

Golightly shrugged. 'Bad tempered, moody ... he would stamp and shout ... he would lock himself in the bathroom for hours on end, especially if he knew me or my mum would want to use the bathroom. I learned to keep out of his way.'

'Friends?'

'None. None that I can remember. Not many people seemed to visit us.'

'Hobbies, pastimes?'

'Up the pub most of the time when he wasn't in the house.'

'Did he go anywhere? I mean, apart from his place of work?'

'Yes. He had another lock-up at the time.'

'Where? Do you remember?'

'It was a car drive away. Not a long drive. Difficult to remember how long, I was very young.'

'Of course.'

'Not very far.'

'Well, less than the distance from Gravely to York?'

'Oh, aye ... much less than that. Out of the village, into the next village.'

'Which direction out of your village?'

'Towards Thorgansby.'

'OK. Did you go as far as Thorgansby?'

'No, still in the fields. There was a propeller on the side of the wall.'

'A propeller?'

'Yes, from an aeroplane. Massive. Dad said it was from a Spitfire in the Second World War. It was bolted on to the outside of the wall, painted white. The propeller, not the wall.'

'OK, this is good.' Yellich reached for his notebook.

Golightly tapped ash off his cigarette. 'I don't like the police, I know where I stand, but I hope you nail him for this one. Murder, that's different. See, if you're a blagger there's good jobs and there's naughty jobs, and murder is a naughty job. I've got mates, you know, in the prison, out of prison; it's like a jungle telegraph. You get him banged up and I'll make sure he gets carved in the showers.'

Maurice Walls drove out of Elmton, glancing to his left as he passed the row of lock-ups, and once again saw his neighbour outside the lock-up with the yellow doors. He was standing there, looking into the garage, as if occupied by thought.

'I don't think this breaches client confidentiality.' Tom Thornton, Mary Golightly's solicitor, had a warm telephone manner, so Hennessey found. 'Particularly since you tell me said client is no more.'

'Definitely no more.'

'Yes, I read the newspapers. It's uncomfortable. Someone you know personally, even if only in a professional capacity: it's still a shock when you read it.'

'I can imagine.'

'Most of our clients don't lead such lives. We are not a criminal law practice. So, how can we help you?'

'Just by confirming that Mrs Mary Golightly was seeking a divorce.'

'Yes, I can confirm that. She was pursuing divorce proceedings.'

Hennessey scribbled on his notepad. 'On what grounds?'

'Mental cruelty and infidelity.'

'Infidelity?'

'Yes.'

'This is interesting. Would you say she had a strong case?'

'Oh, yes. We were going to take him to the cleaners. He would have had to sell the house and give her half the value.'

'So there was substance to her allegation of infidelity?'

'Oh, yes. Mrs Golightly engaged a private detective. He obtained a lot of incriminating photographs of Mr Golightly with his lady friend.'

'Do you know her name?'

'I do, but I am not at liberty to tell you that.'

'Understood.' Hennessey turned to one side as his eye was caught by a group of tourists walking the walls; Japanese, he thought, very excitedly looking about themselves, wearing light blue baseball caps,

about ten persons, youthful, equally balanc-
ed between men and women. 'Could you
furnish me with the name of the private
detective?'

'Well, the agency was Sellers, based in
Harrogate.'

'Sellers, Harrogate.' Hennessey wrote on
his pad.

'They're in the book. All information
about the third party will be furnished by
them.'

'Thanks. Did Mrs Golightly express any
fear of her husband?'

'Not to me. Never indicated that he was
physically violent. I can tell you that divorce
proceedings are long and drawn out, and
Mrs Golightly's manner at the outset and
throughout was what we normally find, low
self-opinion, embarrassed, even ashamed
that it's come to this. A sense that they have
betrayed their family, a fear that they will be
the subject of gossip and the target of point-
ing fingers ... all that was Mrs Golightly's
manner, until very recently. It was as though
a spark had been ignited, a flame rekindled.
She was happy, confident. The divorce

suddenly became the best thing that could happen.'

'Did she tell you why she had a change of attitude?'

'She didn't have to. She'd found someone. It really was as plain as plain could be. They were both being unfaithful to each other, though I am confident that it was Mr Golightly who broke the sanctity of their marriage.'

'And they were living together still?'

'Unusual, but not unknown. They seemed to live separate lives under the same roof.'

'I see. Well, thank you. Sellers?'

'Of Harrogate.'

Nicole Butterworth sat in the upholstered chair, opposite the counsellor, looking out into the garden of the unit.

'It's called "trauma bonding".' The counsellor spoke with a soft voice.

'Trauma bonding?'

'Yes ... when someone has been traumatized and the incident took place at a specific location, people find themselves drawn to that location and go back and revisit it.

People who survived the King's Cross fire all those years ago still return to the underground station. As the years go by, the frequency of their visits becomes less and less ... they are adjusting to the trauma. So maybe you ought to go back there. Could you find the wood?'

'Yes ... I think so. In fact, I know I could.'

'You are doing very well to stay off the alcohol. I know it's a struggle, and one day at a time isn't a lot of fun, but if you drink because of the trauma ... revisiting the wood so that you gain some sense that you control the surroundings ... and would leave on your terms ... it might help.'

'Yes...' Nicole Butterworth nodded her head. 'Yes ... yes, I think that would help. I'll do that.'

Hennessey drove to Harrogate. He took the direct route, the A59, which he believed followed the route of a Roman road, across flat, lush, green country, over the meandering Nidd, through the Hammertons, into Knaresborough and then Harrogate, its nestling neighbour. He pulled into the car park of the Sandford Hotel and entered the building. It had a soft atmosphere and smelled deliciously of percolated coffee. At the reception desk he asked to consult their Yellow Pages and finding Sellers Private Detective Agency, he asked the white-bloused, black-skirted receptionist where Pond Road was.

'Quite near, sir. Out the door, turn right, second left.'

'Thanks.' He showed the receptionist his ID. 'This is police business. Would it be all right if I left my car in your car park? There's plenty of space.'

'I'm sure that would be all right, sir.' A white, toothpaste-selling smile cracked open across a fair and freckled face.

Hennessey left the hotel, squinting his eyes against the glare of the sun, and walked down a narrow main road lined with impressive stone buildings, which at ground floor level were antique shops, expensive-looking restaurants, solicitors' offices, and then took the second turning on the left and into a drab side street of terraced housing and small shops, a pub called the Crown and Anchor. He guessed that, like all Crown and Anchors, the pub derived its name from a petty officer's badge of rank, but as an inland pub, the name was strange. All the Crown and Anchors he had known were in bustling seaports. He found the detective agency easily, helped by a large sign in the window of what was once a small terraced house. He rapped on the black metal door-knocker.

'You're police.' The man who opened the door was middle-aged, a beer belly beneath a blue shirt, a thin leather belt held up dark blue trousers; his feet looked comfortable in sandals. 'I can tell that knock, tap, tap ... tap. The policeman's knock.'

'Yes, I am.' Hennessey showed the man his ID. 'You're Mr Sellers?'

'The one and only.'

'I think you can be of some assistance to us, Mr Sellers.'

Sellers smiled, inclined his head, and stood back and to one side. 'Well, in that case, you'd better come in ... in, out of the sun.'

Sellers's office Hennessey found to be neat

and cramped. It was housed in a small room on the ground floor of the old house, and the neatness seemed to be imposed as a means of coping with the absence of space. Hennessey sat in front of Sellers's desk, which stood against the window. Their conversation would be punctuated by the sound of folk walking down the pavement on the other side of the pane of glass.

'Yes, the Golightly case. I read about it.' Sellers leaned back in his chair, and a serious expression fell over his face, as Hennessey explained the reason for his visit. 'Very sad business.'

'Don't get much sadder.'

'Chopped up into little pieces?'

'We presume; we only recovered one "little piece". So you were hired by Mrs Golightly?'

'Yes.' The answer was short, sharp, to the point.

'So, what did you find out for her? What, that is, that we might be interested in?'

'Well, that's for you to say.' Sellers smiled. Somebody walked heavily across the floor of the room above them. 'The other tenants,'

Sellers explained. 'I rent the bottom half of this house, where the kitchen is ... well, a small compact cooker and a sink and some cupboards, and they have the upstairs rooms. Don't know what they do, sit in front of a computer screen all day, but they seem to generate an income. The toilet is upstairs, so we pass each other on the way up or down. Cheery lads, full of the confidence that is youth. Ah, those were the days ... to have those days again.'

'Private eye work not paying?'

'Not as much as I'd like it to pay. Damn frustrating at times. You wait outside a pub for a couple for a few hours just to lose them at the first traffic lights. Clients want results.'

'Mostly divorce work?'

'Pretty well all my work is divorce work. It's the big agencies that do other stuff, like industrial espionage or fraud. They can insert someone into a company at a low level as an employee; hopefully he'll get invited to take part in whatever scam all the other employees are operating, and so the thing is uncovered. That sort of thing takes time. The mole has to live the life of a company employee. That can be low life and low income, I mean, living in a damp bedsit and walking to work. Not many PIs are prepared to do that, no matter what they're being paid by the agency.'

'I can imagine.'

'But I am a one-man band. All I can do is divorce work, taking incriminating photographs with a telephoto lens, using hire cars or vans so the target never gets to recognize the car that's following him. We don't follow people very often, only at the beginning of the affair. Once we ... once *I* get to know where they tend to go, I can anticipate their movements and get there ahead of them. That's always better anyway, get a good position with my elephant gun—'

'Your what?'

'My telephoto lens. I have a few lenses ... the largest is huge, it was expensive, 600mm with a tripod, cost as much as a good second-hand car or an annual holiday for a family. Tax deductible, of course, but if you have that equipment and you're a quarter of a mile away, to photograph them when they meet, that first embrace, that kiss, well, that's the case complete. Costs a bit, but it benefits the client because he or she can divorce on the grounds of adultery, for a much more favourable settlement than they could if the marriage had simply broken down.'

'Is that what Mrs Golightly wanted?'

'Yes. She got it as well.'

'The divorce? I thought—'

'The evidence. One step at a time, evidence first, favourable divorce settlement second. She got the evidence. Wanted more, but she got what she needed.'

'More?'

'More evidence ... more photographs of Mr G's illicit trysts. I think she wanted them more to convince herself than for evidence against him.'

'I see. Do you mind if I have a look at the photographs?'

'You can have them.' Sellers stood. He walked two or three paces to a filing cabinet, opened the drawer, ran his fingers along the spines of the files, selected one and returned to his desk. He sat down and opened the file. In the pocket of the file were grainy, matt-finished black and white photographs, six in all, showing Terence Golightly Senior in the company of another, younger woman. 'That's about the best one.' Sellers selected one of the photographs and tossed it dismissively across the desk to Hennessey.

Hennessey picked it up, turned it ninety degrees and considered it. It showed Terence Golightly and a young, dark-haired woman in a state of undress, lying in long grass at the edge of a stand of trees. Both Terence Golightly Senior and the young woman were clearly identifiable. 'I see what you mean.'

'They had no idea I was there, eating my sandwiches, watching the trains go by.'

'The trains?' Hennessey looked again at the photograph. The upper parts of the bodies of both persons took up most of the print. It was as if Sellers had been standing over them when he took the photograph. 'How far away were you?'

'About ... about quarter of a mile. They were lying in a field that was above a railway cutting, then there was a road running alongside the railway line, then the hill on which I was concealed just below the skyline.'

'Do you enjoy your job?' Hennessey put the photograph down.

'Yes, actually I do. I am on the side of the wronged party after all. That is the nature of the game...' He paused as a heavy male footfall descended the stairs and walked along the short corridor to the kitchen, whereupon followed sounds of running water and the rattle of mugs. 'Coffee time for those above,' he explained – needlessly, thought Hennessey. He had worked that out for himself. 'Yes, it's the nature of the game. Nobody phones us ... or me up, and says, "I'm committing a crime, I'm defrauding my employers, I'm being unfaithful to my partner, come and photograph me." It's always the other way round. It's the businessmen who can't understand why their company is haemorrhaging and suspect their employees of siphoning money, and want us, the PIs, to uncover it. It's the men and women like Mrs Golightly who come in to see us, often in tears, saying they suspect their husband or wife is playing away from home, and could we help them? We help those who have been dealt an injustice. That's the way I see it, and so, yes, I do enjoy my job.'

'And Mrs Golightly was in tears?'

'Close to, at the outset.'

'At the outset?'

'Yes, when she first came to see me. Latterly, like I said, she was a very happy-looking woman. Dare say it was something to do with the guy and the silver Citroën.'

'Now,' Hennessey said. 'Now I want the identity of not one, but two persons.'

Sellers smiled. 'The first person is called Amanda Holyman. I can let you have the address. The second person, all I can say is that he is male and drives a silver Citroën. A decent-sized Citroën, not a 2CV.'

'You don't know his name?'

'Nope. Or address. I don't spy on my clients. She came here one day, driven by the guy in the Citroën. I gave her a few photographs and she paid her bill up to date. I bill by the month, and then finally, so the client pays over time. It helps them budget; better than hitting them with a massive bill at the end.'

'Sounds reasonable.'

'It seems to be preferred, but they are also told of what progress we have made. It was the last time I saw her. She came to pay for the first four weeks' work and I showed her the photographs. She seemed very pleased, paid by cheque, grabbed the photographs and ran out to the waiting Citroën parked just across the road.' He glanced to his right.

'Did you get a good look at the driver of the Citroën?'

"No, he seemed a little ... uncomfortable. Head turned away, hat pulled down, as though he regretted parking where he did, as though he was not expecting to be seen.'

'That,' said Hennessey, 'is very interesting. Very interesting indeed.' He took out his notebook. 'Amanda Holyman?'

Sellers gave an address in York.

'Anything about the car or driver you'd recognize again?'

'The car had a used look about it.'

'Used? As in many previous owners?'

'No ... I mean used as in it seemed to be a

car that worked for its living, not a car to commute in, or to run to the shops in, but a car that had a job to do ... not a salesman's car either, it wasn't clean enough. More like an unmarked police vehicle or a taxi ... but it wasn't a taxi. Taxi drivers in this town don't drive Citroëns.'

'They don't in York, come to think of it. Vauxhalls or Japanese cars ... but not Citroëns. Too Francophobic, I expect.'

'As good as any,' Sellers grinned. 'You know, people who know me often tell me that I suffer from Francophobia, being a pathological hatred of the French.'

'I know, it's a very English characteristic.'

'Well, whenever that is said to me I always reply by saying there's no suffering involved, it's a lovely state of mind, and it's not pathological either.'

Hennessey laughed. 'So, a car, as you say, that ferries its owner about as part of the owner's daily life, but not as gleaming as a salesman's car.'

'I'd say. That was my observation and my work does make me observant. But there was nothing distinctive about the car, no dents or other damage, no roof rack, had an aerial.'

'Do you know what type of Citroën?'

'No, but if you leave me a contact number, I'll call you when I do know.'

Hennessey's eyes narrowed. 'She's not coming back.'

'I know, but if I see an identical model I'll make a note of the model number or name and bell you with it.'

'Of course.' Again Hennessey felt embarrassed at his slowness of wit ... in earlier years ... retirement was indeed beckoning. He fished into his wallet and handed Sellers his card.

'Micklegate Bar,' Sellers read the card. 'Yes, I know the police station there ... and this number is the switchboard?'

'Yes, just ask for me or leave a message.'

'Will do. I'll go for a stroll this afternoon, get me out of this box, it gets claustrophobic at times, but I have to stay at home as it were because lots of my clients are "walk ins".'

'Just come in off the street?'

'Yes. Phoning can be difficult if you are in

a stressed marriage, and being up the side street...' Sellers paused as the heavy footfall was heard leaving the kitchen and negotiating the stairs. 'Someone's got his coffee. Being hidden away up a side street means that people have a certain anonymity and being in Harrogate also helps ... most of my clients live not in this town.'

'As with Mrs Golightly?'

'Indeed. It would be difficult for her if she was seen going into a private detective agency in York, but a short drive to Harrogate confers more secrecy.'

'I can understand that.'

'But I can't stay in all the time. It is hot and fairly airless in here. I don't like the sun, but I will allow myself an hour. It's lunchtime soon...' He held up a sign which read 'Out to lunch'. 'I'll put this in the window. Won't lose a deal of custom. Times are slow anyway. I am convinced the divorce rate climbs during bad weather.'

'Children's behaviour worsens in blustery weather, so you might be correct.'

'Really?'

'So I am told. My sergeant's good wife

used to be a schoolteacher. She once told me that teachers know they are going to have class control problems if the trees are swaying backwards and forwards in the mornings, as the staff and pupils journey to school.'

'Interesting ... so weather can influence human behaviour?'

'Seems so. Now, the occupant of the car?'

'Male, forties, didn't want to be seen. Not unusual, though, not when liaising with married women, but that's part of the fun.'

'Is it?'

'Oh, yes.' Sellers smiled. 'As I get older, women in sour marriages are becoming to be the only fruit. But there's fun in the secrecy and the discretion, the creating of smokescreens, laying of false trails. Mobile phones are the unfaithful spouse's best friend. "Just approaching Manchester now, dear," said the lady as we pulled into the hotel car park in Scarborough. You can put yourself anywhere in the world with a mobile phone and be anywhere else, and you can also switch them off so you can't be called at inopportune moments.'

'I can see that. Don't like using them. I have one. I have found I need it, but keep it switched off most of the time. I still believe that they fry your brains. Anything else about the man in the plain, dent-free Citroën?'

'Casual but smart dress. It was Saturday that she called, so you might perhaps deduce from that that the driver works normal office hours. It would be more useful if she had called mid-week because then that would have meant her man friend was a shift worker. You could have narrowed the field down more that way, but all I can say is that he probably isn't a shift worker.'

'Helps. Every little bit helps. You mention-ed a hat...' Hennessey probed.

'A cap. But not a pigeon fancier's cloth cap, a member's enclosure at York Race courses flat cap.'

'Middle class?'

'Yes, professional type. The car ... back to the car.'

'Yes?'

'Not a distinctive car. Had a client once

173

whose better half was a barrister, his car was a real sledge, a big Mercedes. He needed it for the distances he had to drive ... one Crown Court one week, another the week after.' Sellers opened the palm of his hand. 'That sort of usage.'

'Yes, my son is a barrister, he has a BMW for that same reason.'

'You must be proud.'

'I am.'

'What parent wouldn't be? Anyway, this car was not a distance car; it didn't say "distance". It said "local journeys only".'

'So, a visiting nurse, a doctor...?'

'Yes, that sort of thing ... a business man who doesn't travel away from the town he works in.'

'Got you. I have the image,' Hennessey smiled. 'Thanks. It's been a great help. You said I could keep the photographs?'

'Yes.' Sellers nodded solemnly. 'She won't need them, will she? Not now.' He paused. 'And I won't get paid. That's an occupational hazard I haven't encountered before.'

It was Wednesday, 12.10 hours.

Yorkshire baked under a relentless sun. Hennessey did not feel like eating even a light meal. Driving out of Harrogate, away from Sellers's agency, he stopped at the first garage he encountered, filled his car up with petrol and added a measure of oil and radiator water. P.O.W.E.R., he had once been told to check them daily: Petrol, Oil, Water, Electricity, Rubber. The tyres looked well-inflated and the electricity clearly worked, so it was just the P.O.W. of it. He also bought a ready-made sandwich and a bottle of mineral water; it was all he wanted on such a hot day. He drove his car away from the petrol pumps to a corner of the forecourt and stood by his car eating the snack as the traffic on the A59 hummed past in both directions. Except the army Land Rovers, he noticed. When they drove past in fast moving convoys of six or seven vehicles, their tyres gave off a high-pitched sound, created, he was once told, by having chunkier, deep tread tyres. Beyond the A59 and on either side of him were yellow fields of oilseed rape, and above, a high canopy of blue. The sandwich and mineral water consumed, he continued his journey to the 'Famous and Faire', to the address that had been supplied by Sellers, being the home of Amanda Holyman.

The address was Holgate: rows of terraced houses, with washing strung across the street and motorcycles chained to lamp-posts. It was an area of York the tourists do not see. The Holyman house revealed itself to be a green-painted house with cream trim, and Amanda Holyman and George Hennessey saw each other at the same time. She saw a tall, middle-aged man with silver hair protruding beneath a panama hat, a lightweight summer jacket, light, pale blue summer trousers and brown shoes. She thought 'stranger with a reason to be in this street'. He saw a young woman, dark-haired, cheesecloth blouse, denim jeans, barefoot, sitting on the step of the terraced house, dragging on a cigarette. They held eye contact with each other as the distance between them closed until Hennessey stood just two feet from her and said, 'Miss

Holyman?'

The young woman looked up, shielding her eyes from the glare of the sun. 'Who wants to know?'

'Police.' Hennessey showed her his ID.

'Well, yes, I'm Amanda Holyman.'

'I'd like to talk to you please, ask a few questions.'

She shrugged her shoulders, dogged the nail and flicked the butt into the gutter. 'Why not? Nothing better to do.' She stood. 'Was at a peace camp once, last summer, outside Menwith Hill tracking station.'

'Oh, yes?'

'Had tents and CND signs and these motorists kept passing and yelling, "Haven't you anything better to do?", and we'd look at each other and say, "Well, frankly, no." Come in.'

Hennessey smiled as he followed her into the dim interior of the house. It was, he found, a 'back to back' house, and so he stepped from the street into the living room. It was pleasantly cool inside. Amanda Holyman sank into an armchair and folded one leg up underneath her.

'Take a pew.' She extended an upturned palm to the other vacant chair. Hennessey did not close the door behind him, sensing that Amanda Holyman wished it to be left open.

'Well,' he sat in the chair. It was old, very old, but he felt exceedingly comfortable. He felt he didn't sit in it, so much as was partially swallowed by it. 'I understand you know Mr Terence Golightly?'

The young woman looked at Hennessey but didn't reply. She seemed to Hennessey to be surprised by the question.

'Well, I know you know him. I know you are romantically involved.'

'That's not a crime.'

'No, and in a sense, it is not our concern, except when it becomes germane.'

'To the murder inquiry?'

'Yes.'

'Terence phoned me. He told me he was being suspected of his wife's murder. He said we should let things cool down for a while. Wait till things blow over.'

'He sounds confident.'

'Why shouldn't he be? He didn't kill her.'

'You know that, do you?'

'He's not a violent man. Selfish ... wants his own way and tends to get it ... a bit of a control freak ... not a very sensitive lover, taking pleasure more than giving it, a bit insensitive, but not violent.'

'Strangely enough, murderers often are not violent. It's quite true. Often the act of murder is the only violent act, the only known violent act, and the only known crime the murderer has committed. That is especially true if the crime is motivated by passion. So how long have you been involved with Mr Golightly?'

'About a year.'

'He's a lot older than you.'

Amanda Holyman smiled, 'Yes ... isn't he lucky? Most middle-aged men can only look at university students, but Terence can do more than that. And does. About three times a week.'

'You are a student?' Hennessey knew what she meant about middle-aged men only being able to look at female university students. Again the realization of his advancing years pierced him like an arrow.

'Was. Just taken my finals. I've registered for postgraduate work dependent upon my results. They're out any day now.'

'You're not from Yorkshire?'

'Cor blimey, love a duck. You can tell can you, me old china? Naw, from the East End, darlin...' She emphasized an East End of London accent, but it clearly came very naturally to her. 'Bethnal Green,' she added, pronouncing it 'Befnal Gween'. 'So, lucky old Terence Golightly, not only is he a middle-aged father of a villain but his twenty-two-year-old bit on the side is an East End girl ... best girls in the world, East End girls, London's roses, me old cock, London's roses.'

'Was your relationship going anywhere?' Hennessey smiled at her spirit.

'Like marriage, you mean?'

'Yes, I mean like marriage.'

Amanda Holyman laughed. 'Don't be daft. No, it had gone.' She shrugged. 'Well, if I get my 2:1 and the PhD course ... it could go a bit further. I was the instigator, you see. I put an ad in the Yorkshire Post: "Sugar baby seeks sugar daddy". He paid the rent on this house so I don't have to share it, and he calls round three times a week.'

'And takes you into the country,' thought Hennessey, but didn't remark on it. He thought it irrelevant, and he didn't think that this London rose would want to know she had been photographed by a man with a camera and a 600mm lens from a distance of a quarter of a mile.

'It meant I could give everything to my course. No relationship to get in the way of brainwork, no money worries, because his lordship took care of the rent. I was hoping for a lawyer or a doctor, but Terence is what I got.'

'So his wife didn't stand in the way of anything?'

'No. Definitely. Unless Terence began to fantasize along those lines, but we never planned for permanence. I was only ever his mistress, and I was only ever going to be his mistress.'

'Very well ... what impression did you have of his marriage?'

'Well, he used to refer to his wife as "the

Gestapo" ... I think that tells us both a lot.'

'Certainly does.' Hennessey raised an eyebrow. '"The Gestapo", that's very strong.'

'Don't get stronger. There was real hatred there. It was in his eyes, frightened me.'

'Did he ever talk of wanting to kill her?'

'No, he didn't. He seemed happy that the divorce was proceeding. How could two people be getting divorced and yet still live in the same house?'

'It's unusual,' Hennessey found himself repeating Thornton's remark, 'but not unknown.'

'They slept separately, at least that was something, I mean, something I could understand ... but living together when you're divorcing ... that's heavy.'

'Did he mention his first wife to you?'

'Yes, she disappeared.' Amanda Holyman's jaw sagged. 'You surely don't suspect him ... blimey ... when will this end?'

'We suspect much in cases like this, Miss Holyman. Can't afford not to.'

'He never said anything that made me think anything of it. He seemed to resent her, talked about her leaving him with a young boy, as though she'd walked off with a fancy man ... but like I said, we were never anything but a sugar daddy and his baby girl. Not the sort of relationship where innermost secrets would be divulged.'

'Indeed.' Hennessey stood. 'I do hope you get your 2:1, Miss Holyman, but if you do, you might like to consider finding another sugar daddy.'

'I think I might,' she replied quietly. 'I think I might.'

'What are you studying? Just out of interest.'

'Me, duck? Divinity, duck.'

It was Wednesday, 13.35 hours.

Five

Wednesday, 3 June,
14.00 hours – 16.30 hours
*in which the officers are shown a bone and learn
more of the antecedents of Terence Golightly.*

The first bone was shown to the officers. The rest they found.

Hennessey and Yellich drove out to Gravely and then followed the road towards Thorgansby. The road drove confidently in a straight line between lush fields and pastures of green with copses in full summer foliage, breaking up the flat landscape, as the sun beat down relentlessly from a clear blue sky. Close to Thorgansby, Yellich pointed to a building but said nothing.

'I see it,' Hennessey whispered, looking at the building, on one wall of which was mounted an aircraft's propeller.

Yellich slowed the car and turned into the premises of the building and read the sign above the door. 'Jas. Stansfield, Engineers.' The door of the premises was open; men in overalls were to be seen toiling. One looked up from the lathe he was working at and approached Hennessey and Yellich.

'Can I help you, gentlemen?' He wiped his hands on an oily cloth, as he spoke. He was youthful, he seemed keen, and there was an alertness in his eyes.

'Mr Stansfield?' Hennessey got out of the car. Yellich did likewise.

'Well, I'm one of them.'

Hennessey looked at the sign. 'Mr James Stansfield?'

'Well, I'm still one of them, but I think it's my father you want to speak to. He's the boss. I'm young James. He's old James, my brother is just David.'

'I see ... well, where is old James?'

'In the office. I'll ask him to come down. It's the police, isn't it?'

'Yes.'

'Thought so ... something about you. That, and the fact most of our customers arrive wearing overalls. But I'll go and get my father.'

'We don't mind coming to see him.'

'Not in clothes like that. It's mucky in there. Believe me, gentlemen, you are better off out here. Won't be a minute.' He walked smartly away, almost at a run, leaving Hennessey and Yellich to the heat and the birdsong and the sound of high-pitched whining and the knocking of metal on metal from within the premises of 'Jas. Stansfield, Engineers'. A few moments later a second man emerged from the building and approached the officers. He was, it was clear to see, an older version of the man who had offered a warm welcome. Clearly 'old James'.

'Mr Stansfield?' Hennessey asked.

'Yes. That's me.' He was in his fifties, bald, spreading at the waist, clad in a boiler suit; hands with short, stubby fingers, which were caked in oil and grease. He held them up. 'You'll forgive me if I don't shake hands?'

'Of course.' Hennessey smiled.

'How can I help you?'

'How long have you had these premises, Mr Stansfield?'

'Had? Well, I own them, not rent ... about ten years, possibly a little more.'

'Were the premises empty when you moved in?' Hennessey glanced around the workshop; metal beams, a high ceiling with a series of opaque skylights.

'Yes. No one here. Picked up the keys from the letting agency.'

'No ... I meant no tools, equipment, documents ... anything like that?'

'No, nothing. Not even an old calendar hanging on the wall.'

'Well, I ask because we are really interested in an event which might have taken place here before you became the owner.'

'A death?'

'Possibly. Why do you ask?'

'There's a presence in the workshop.' He indicated the building behind him with an upturned thumb. 'Never see anything, nothing moves, but from about five o'clock onwards, there's a sense that someone is watching you. "Bertie", we call him. A few blokes have walked away, not wanting to work here, but most don't mind, you get used to it. Whenever anyone feels that they're being watched they say, "Hello, Bertie". The presence seems to like that.'

'You think?'

'It's the feeling you just get. Again, a lot of the blokes say the same thing. Once they say, "Hello, Bertie," the presence seems to wander away and a minute later one of the other blokes will say, "Hello Bertie", as if he feels he's being watched. But that's only after five o'clock ... sometimes we work late, you see ... if we have a deadline to meet, for instance.'

'I see. Well, if we are right, if our information is correct, the presence might be that of a female, it might be "Beatrice", not "Bertie".'

'Really?' Colour drained from Stansfield's face. 'Er ... would this lady have been chopped up? I presume you are talking about a murder. I mean, you wouldn't be here if "Beatrice" had died accidentally or of natural causes.'

'"Probably", and "yes", are the answers to your question, in that order. Why do you mention being chopped up?'

'Because there's a bone sticking up out of

the concrete over there.' He pointed to his left, and to Hennessey and Yellich's right.

'A bone!'

'Yes.'

'You are not suspicious of it?'

'We always thought it was a bit of animal bone ... we never connected it to "Bertie" or "Beatrice". I'll show you.' He turned and walked to his left across the expanse of concrete. Hennessey and Yellich followed. In the corner, Stansfield stopped and tapped a small protuberance from the concrete bed. 'That's it. I discovered it by accident. Trod on it.'

Yellich knelt and examined it more closely. 'It's bone all right, boss.'

'Never thought anything of it. Fella I bought the premises off, he told me the last owner had put the concrete down on the front and left-hand side of the workshop and that he'd been a butcher who had gone into the wholesale food industry. I presumed it was an animal bone.'

'Fair enough.' Hennessey paused. 'We're going to have to dig this bit of bone out. Have it examined. If it turns out to be human, the whole of this concrete apron will have to come up, bit by bit.'

'Oh, it'll be human all right.' Stansfield shook his head and looked down.

'Why do you say that, sir?'

'Because for weeks now we've been receiving hate mail from the bank manager, a contract we've been pinning our hopes on has been cancelled, and it's my experience that just when you don't think things can get worse – they do. So, on that basis alone, you have my guarantee that that bone will be human. How will you extract it?'

'Dig it out with a pneumatic drill. We'll dig round it ... take the lump of concrete to Wetherby.'

'Wetherby?'

'That's where the forensic science lab we use is located.'

'I see. Do the police have to do that?'

'Not necessarily, why?'

'Just that I could save you time. We've got a pneumatic in the shop. I'll get David onto it. He's not got a job at the moment.'

'That would be very useful. Thank you.'

'Aye...' sighed Stansfield as he ambled

back towards the workshop. Watching him go, Hennessey was never more grateful for his years of secure employment and the inflation-proof pension that was soon to be his. Yellich too pondered that whilst he could be dismissed from the police force for some misdeed, he need never fear redundancy.

'Don't know how lucky we are, boss.'

'I was thinking the same.' Hennessey spoke softly, again pleased that his working life was nearing its end. Thus far he hadn't messed up, thus far his pension was his, but he was aware that for him the ides of March had come ... but not gone.

Thirty minutes later, Hennessey and Yellich were driving to Wetherby with Hennessey in the passenger seat nursing, on his lap, a lump of concrete as large as a dinner plate, he estimated, that had a small amount of bone sticking out of it, grey and sun-bleached and cracked with frost, wrapped up in a plastic bag. 'It's only Asda,' had smiled James 'old James' Stansfield. 'Can't run to Marks and Spencer these days.' But the Asda bag did admirably, easily accommodating the piece of concrete. Later still, having deposited it at the forensic science laboratory, and having had it cross-referred to the crime number of the Mary Golightly investigation for the attention of DCI Hennessey, Yellich asked, 'What now, boss?'

Hennessey glanced at his watch. 'Back to Gravely. I think we'll have another chat with Terence Golightly.'

It was Wednesday, 15.42 hours.

She had found that some movement was possible, a little, but only a little, and she exploited it as much as she could. It gave her a sense of self, it afforded a little measure of self control, but it did not assuage the fear, the dread, the sense of helplessness, or hopelessness. It was not death she feared, she had found, but it was the when of it, and the how of it.

'So what do you think, skipper?' Yellich swilled the tea around his mug. 'Bring in Golightly senior, lean on him...'

'Not yet. Let's wait until the boffins confirm that the bones in the cement are those of the first Mrs Golightly. They can do that easily enough by comparing young Terence's DNA with the DNA they can extract from the bone fragments. If it is a match, we more than bring him in to lean on him, we bring him in and charge him with murder.'

'Moving slowly,' Yellich said, coldly.

Hennessey paused. He glanced at Yellich. It was a look Yellich had not seen before ... a look of irritation. 'Don't push things, Yellich. I am the senior man, this will be done at my pace.'

Yellich too paused. He held eye contact with Hennessey. He felt a surge of anger. 'With respect, sir ... we could move at a faster pace ... I would, if I was in charge.'

'Well you are not in charge. Kindly remember that.'

Hennessey's phone rang. He let it ring twice before he picked it up. 'DCI Hennessey. Ah, yes, Mr Sellers...' Hennessey glanced at Yellich and mouthed, 'The private detective'. 'Yes ... good of you to phone. A C4? Excellent. Thank you. Silver? Yes, got that. Thank you again.' He replaced the receiver a second time in the space of a minute. 'The private eye, he's certain that is the car that brought Mrs Golightly ... the second Mrs Golightly, whose thigh we are in possession of, thanks to the refuse collector who found it, grubbing away in other folk's rubbish. You know, I can understand him, Yellich. A hard job.'

'Think so, boss?' Yellich avoided eye contact. 'It's very clean these days. Out of doors, wet weather clothing provided for the winter, your mind is your own, no office politics from which you can't escape, and the knowledge that your job is vital. It isn't doctors that keep us healthy; it's refuse collectors and folk who work in sewage farms. They work for peanuts, but we are healthy because of them.'

'Generally, but I am pleased we have our excellent doctors. But I meant that if you knew that treasure was yours if you found it ... despite what the management might think, you'd have quite a motivation to work ... quite a motivation to turn up for work. Working for profit or personal gain, there's much to be said for it. I can understand the motivation of the likes of Mr Fenby. Was that his name? I can understand why he turns in for work at the crack of dawn.'

Yellich nodded. 'Yes, I can too, boss. I don't like it, but I can understand it.'

'Yes ... but to get back on track. That was the private detective. The car that brought the second Mrs Golightly to his premises was a Citroën C4.'

'That's quite a new make.'

'So I believe. A silver one, and Mrs Golightly was looking radiant. Apparently.'

'So, someone who owns, or has access to, a silver Citroën C4, was making Mrs Golightly a very happy woman at the time of her death. Middle class by all accounts ... according to Mr Sellers ... interesting, that, elevated above her in terms of social class ... a charming man, a knight in shining armour rescuing her from a poisonous marriage ... there's more than a few women in England who'd love for a man like that to walk into their lives. Such women make easy prey if said knight isn't as chivalrous as he might first appear. And that man couldn't have been Terence Golightly. No C4, and he doesn't seem to be the sort of man that would make any woman happy for long.'

'Another predator, you think?'

'It's looking that way, sir. Very solemn.' Yellich's voice had an edge to it.

Nicole Butterworth located the wood without difficulty, a short bus ride out of York, then a walk. A wood? More of a copse really, less than half the size of a hockey pitch. An old copse and a new copse at the same time, this ancient tree, that oak sapling, which would still not be approaching maturity when she would have long since passed from this life. She wondered what other events had these trees witnessed? What other events would they witness? Acts of love, acts of hate? Here amid the foliage and the birdsong, here in the shade, humans have done, and humans would do. She found the location, those few square feet where her life was very nearly robbed. Ah, yes ... yes ... there it was ... the stone ... that selfsame stone, now covered in moss. She pondered about whether to take it home. She decided against it. It was not the sort of keepsake she wanted, or needed. Besides some other, future lass, a lass not yet born, might have a similar use for it. She remained in the copse for an hour and then slowly walked away, following the path she had some years earlier run along in a fearful panic. She thought the counsellor correct: she was recovering control of the dreadful location and leaving on her terms ... and the need to block it all out with alcohol excess was reducing. She would revisit the copse. Again and again.

Hennessey and Yellich returned to Micklegate Bar Police Station. Yellich phoned his wife, then went home. Hennessey, reluctant to return to an empty house, save for his dog, walked down the CID corridor to Commander Sharkey's office, hoping the good commander was working late. He was.

It was a rare sight in Hennessey's experience for Sharkey to smile, and even rarer for him to laugh. Sharkey was, Hennessey had always found, a serious-minded man, young for his rank, concerned almost to the point of obsession about corruption in the police force in general and Micklegate Bar in particular. Sharkey, with his neat desk, with photographs of himself in the army and later the Royal Hong Kong Police, Sharkey of single-minded, serious-minded attitude, a man not at all given to humour. Yet, yet, on that Wednesday evening when Hennessey had finished relating the progress into the investigation into the murder of Mrs Mary Golightly, a smile appeared to form, and then a short laugh.

'You mean, George,' Sharkey said, 'you mean that Terence Golightly is not in the frame for the murder of his wife, but upon investigation you uncovered one earlier disappearance of a woman which he is now implicated in and which he might have got away with if someone else, probably someone with a silver Citroën, hadn't probably murdered his wife?'

'Yes, sir.'

It was then that Sharkey laughed. Not a long, loud bellow, but a short, soft, gentle laugh ... a chuckle, and then he said, 'Well, that's rich. There's justice for you.'

'It's rather ironic ... I'll give you that, sir.'

'You haven't arrested him yet?'

'Not yet, sir, he's not going anywhere. He's not a part of the underworld, there's nowhere he can go. The results of the bone we found in the cement at Stansfield Engineering will come back soon. If the DNA tests prove that it's from his first wife ... which it will ... so my waters tell me.'

'The waters of an old copper, eh, George?'

'Not often wrong, sir. Anyway, then we'll gently fondle his collar and charge him with the murder of the first Mrs Golightly.'

'Indeed.'

'Indeed, sir. Just leaves us the murder of Mrs Mary Golightly. The only lead there is is a man with a Citroën, a silver C4.'

'Managing the workload, George? Not thinking of moving to a desk job just to ease off in the final stretch?'

'No, thank you, sir.' Hennessey stood. 'I concluded my National Service by stepping off a destroyer, and I want to conclude my service with the police by walking out of my office in the CID corridor, not from archives or from escorting children across the road.'

★ ★ ★

So he had been playing games. She had now been given food and fluid. And silence. Plenty of silence. He never spoke to her. Not a word. Fed her, gave her water, took the plastic bucket away, returned with a clean and empty bucket, closed the door, locked it, left her alone.

'Don't know about Yellich.' Hennessey and Louise D'Acre strolled arm in arm along the country lane, enjoying each other's company.

'I thought you valued him?' She glanced at him.

'I do ... he's a good sergeant but he's getting pushy ... I don't like that. We've all got a part to play, he knows that, but recently he's been forcing the pace ... I feel as if he's trying to take over ... pushing me to my retirement.'

'I'm sure that's not the case.'

'Well, it damn well feels like it. Something is coming between us. I am certain.'

The rest of the walk continued in silence.

Six

Saturday, 6 June,
11.00 hours – Tuesday, 16.45 hours
in which the police use a ploy.

James Stansfield could only watch with growing despair, and a growing sense of injustice.

The bone fragment had been examined by Dr D'Acre and the forensic science laboratory at Wetherby, who had both pronounced it to be human. Age, sex, ethnicity were undetermined, but it was definitely human. That information awaited DCI Hennessey when he arrived at Micklegate Bar Police Station that Saturday morning. One hour later, he and Sergeant Yellich, a uniformed sergeant and fifteen constables descended on Jas. Stansfield Engineering and, to Stansfield's dismay, requested all motor vehicles be removed from the concrete area surrounding the building. With the assistance of five pneumatic drills, operated by the stronger police constables, the concrete apron was carefully taken up, square metre by square metre. As the operation proceeded, with each small piece of concrete being carefully examined, the concrete began to give up its grim secrets. Fragments of bone were discarded, each small, each clearly sawn or hacked from a larger bone, each piece placed with reverence in a black plastic container, which stood at the edge of the concrete, guarded by a female police constable, who stood barely moving under the fierce sun and cloudless blue sky. Hennessey and Yellich stood supervising the operation. The employees of Jas. Stansfield looked on with excited curiosity. The Stansfields themselves, especially James the elder, looked on with a wealth of emotions, none particularly comfortable.

'Shall we arrest Golightly?' Yellich turned to Hennessey. 'He'll hear about this activity, it might put him to flight. I know that he can't go anywhere ... he won't be able to stay submerged for long, but we'd better stop him before he goes.' He raised his voice so as to be heard over the noise of the drills.

'Are you presuming to do my job for me, Detective Sergeant?' Hennessey turned on Yellich.

'Not at all, sir ... I just thought...'

'Well, I'd be obliged if you didn't think, when you know very well that I am the senior man.'

'With respect, I have an opinion too. I have a say.' Yellich's voice was firm. 'I have a say,' he repeated calmly, 'and I say we arrest Golightly ... he's likely to run. We have to move and we have to move fast.'

Hennessey remained silent. He had to concede that Yellich had a good point. 'Yes ... all right, who will you take with you?'

'One of the constables from here, sir. I can return him once Golightly's in the cells.'

'Yes, do that.' Once again, as happened lately, he noticed Yellich, the younger officer, and much junior in rank, had taken the initiative and suggested something that he, Hennessey, should have ordered. He was getting old, retirement did indeed beckon, and Commander Sharkey's offer of a desk job might have its merits after all. As Yellich collected one of the constables, who seemed to Hennessey to be more than happy to leave the hot, dusty work of chipping concrete away from bone fragments, he walked over to where James Stansfield stood with his two sons. 'I am sorry about this, but it has to be done.'

'I can understand that,' James Stansfield spoke softly. 'I wouldn't want the concrete there anyway, not with bits of someone in it. To think that we've been walking on that ... it will have to be re-laid ... the insurance won't cover this ... it's just going to be more expense when we're struggling as it is. Tarmac might be cheaper but it wouldn't last like concrete. Concrete gets harder over time.'

'Didn't know that.'

'Yes, for the first sixty years after it's laid it gets continually harder, then it sets and remains set for ... well, centuries ... before it decays. The concrete round those bones is harder now than when it was laid.' Stansfield pondered the concrete. 'Always thought it had a roughshod looking quality about it ... wasn't a professional job, it has cracks in places. Didn't keep a wet edge, you see. If you want it laid properly you have to keep a wet edge, but if one man was doing this and inserting bits of bone as he went, the concrete would be shallow, only two or three inches thick, then it would have taken him a few days to do this. He would have had to do what he could in a day, then returned the next day to carry on, but by then his previous day's work would be hardened, he would have lost his wet edge and the new concrete wouldn't bond properly with the previous day's concrete ... that's why you have the cracks.' James Stansfield forced a smile. 'But this is expense I don't need. Glad it's going, though. All those years and there's been a body in that stuff.'

'Yes,' Hennessey said.

'Strewth...' Stansfield looked at the area of concrete, by then half turned to rubble. 'All things considered, I'm glad to see the back of it, very glad.'

★ ★ ★

The twin cassettes of the tape recorder spun slowly. The red recording light glowed.

'I am DCI Hennessey. The time is ... two thirty-five p.m., the date is the sixth of June, the location of this interview is Number Two interview suite at Micklegate Bar Police Station, York. I am now going to ask the other people in the room to identify themselves.'

'Detective Sergeant Yellich, Micklegate Bar Police Station.'

'Courtney Smyles of Grayson McDonald and Plowright, St Leonard's Place, York.' She was a middle-aged woman, slender, short hair, smelling too heavily of perfume for Hennessey's taste. She sat as most solicitors do, Hennessey had come to observe, when in situations like this, pen poised over notebook, mind focused, total concentration.

Terence Golightly glowered at Hennessey and then mumbled, 'Terence Golightly.'

'A little more clearly please, Mr Golightly,' Hennessey asked.

Golightly looked sullen, thought Hennessey, as though he could not understand why he should be where he was, as though he could see nothing wrong with murder, as though he thought, 'All right, I did it, but it was twenty years ago.' Then he growled, 'Terence Golightly,' not as loud as Hennessey would have liked, but sufficiently loud so as to be audible and clearly recorded.

'You understand why you are here, Mr Golightly?'

'Please make it a question, Chief Inspector,' Courtney Smyles asked. 'The tape recorder doesn't pick up question marks.'

'Do you understand why you are here, Mr Golightly?' Hennessey complied with Courtney Smyles's request and, indeed, was happy to do so. If convictions are going to be secure, the whole procedure must be by the book. He was acutely aware that the strongest of evidence can count for nothing if procedural errors are allowed to happen.

'Yes.' Again the reply was growled. Golightly held his head down and to one side. He didn't look at Hennessey or Yellich, or even his solicitor, whom he had specially asked to represent him as dictated by the

Police and Criminal Evidence Act. It was as though he was wishing himself to be a long way away, as though he was detaching himself from the present.

'And is it the case that you have been cautioned?'

'Yes.' Golightly nodded to Yellich. 'He said the magic words ... I don't have to say anything but it will harm my defence if I do not mention, when questioned, anything I may later rely on in court. Is that it?'

'Yes, that's it.'

'Prefer the old one, "You do not have to say anything but anything you do say will be taken down and may be given in evidence".'

'So do we.' Hennessey smiled. 'Or so did we. We've got used to the new caution and there are sufficient constables now who have known nothing else but the present caution.'

'I can understand.'

Hennessey sensed Golightly was trying to steer the conversation away from the reason why he had been arrested and cautioned, but at least he was talking. Nonetheless, he decided to focus on the interview. 'There's no point in prolonging this, so let's cut to the chase, shall we?' He glanced up at the opaque pane of glass that was set high in the wall and was the only source of natural light in the room; the main illumination was provided by a filament bulb concealed behind a perspex filter. The floor was covered by hessian carpet, brown in colour; the desk around which they sat was darkly polished pine, the chairs were plastic on metal legs; the walls were painted dark orange. The ceiling was of foam tiles. 'We are digging up the concrete apron which surrounds the workshop presently housing the premises of James Stansfield Engineering, premises once owned by yourself at the time the concrete was laid.'

'So?'

'Did you lay the concrete?'

'No comment.'

'A bone was found in the concrete ... it was protruding. It was removed, it was identified as human, tests showed it belonged to your first wife, Mrs Rosemary Golightly.'

'So?'

'More bones have been discovered as we have dug up the concrete, all in very small pieces. Terence, you're on a hook, there's no point in wriggling ... you're just working the hook in deeper.'

'You think?'

'Yes, I think.'

'I'd like to talk to my lawyer. In private.'

'Very well.' Hennessey reached for the on/off switch. 'The time is two forty-seven p.m. The interview is being halted to allow Mr Golightly to consult with his legal adviser.' He switched off the machine, the red light dimmed and died, the spools stopped turning. Hennessey stood. 'How long do you need?'

'Ten minutes,' Golightly answered, and surprised Hennessey by smiling and adding, 'please.'

Hennessey and Yellich stood by the hot drinks vending machine.

'I don't like this.'

'It's a bit bad,' Yellich agreed. 'I always go for tea from such machines ... safer than the coffee.'

'No ... I mean in there.' Hennessey nodded to the interview room. 'His manner changed so suddenly, his eyes brightened up. Did you notice?'

'I didn't.'

'I did.' Hennessey sipped the hot drink from the white plastic beaker. 'He's got a trick up his sleeve.'

'But what can it be, skipper? You're right, we've got him, it's one hell of a secure conviction. He laid the concrete; the bones were put there by him.'

'Depends what is cooking up in his mind. There's a cunning about that man. He's sullen with us, but I bet he can turn on the charm.'

'Like the "False Knight", you mean?'

'Who is he?'

'The Devil in English mythology. Our Sara used to teach English at a secondary school, has a degree in English Literature, clever lass. Anyway, she once told me about reference to the "False Knight" in medieval writings, a favoured disguise for the Devil. Charming, courteous, well spoken, well mannered, deadly.'

'Yes ... that's the idea. Anyway, we'll soon

see what web of lies and deceit they have hatched between them.'

It was Saturday, 15.02 hours.

Tuesday, 9th June
10.00 hours – 14.30 hours

'It's like a game of double or quits.' The CPS solicitor leaned back in his chair. He was grim-faced and held eye contact with Hennessey. Behind him, Hennessey could see the skyline of the city of York, a mingle of old and new buildings. 'I know the Crown Prosecution Service is known in the police canteens as the "Criminal Protection Service" but the plain truth is that he and his solicitor are in effect offering what our cousins in the United States would call a plea-bargain. As you know, we don't plea-bargain in the UK, but that's what it amounts to.' He patted the reports that lay on his desk. 'If we charge him with murder he has a good chance of being acquitted. If we accept his story about accidental death and panic, we could charge him with un-lawful disposal of the dead ... four years, out in just over two.'

'You think acquittal is likely?' Hennessey asked.

'Not only do I think it likely, I doubt if I could get it passed by the great and the good upstairs. There is no medical evidence of foul play, is there?' He turned to Louise D'Acre.

'None.' Louise D'Acre had sat quietly through the meeting, not offering information, but speaking fully when addressed. 'As I said in my report, the bones have been broken into small pieces, with a saw or a cleaver. All show fire damage, which is consistent with his account of the death, but all those cuts and carbonization were most probably post-mortem. The skull is missing, as I reported, but there seems to be sufficient bones for one adult female. I have asked Wetherby to check for poisons but that is unlikely to be the cause of death. He probably banged her over the head, then cut the head off and dropped it into the Aire. A skull won't float, it would have sunk like a stone, and if this happened so long ago, it will have worked its way into the mud now.'

'Aye,' Yellich growled. 'If it hasn't been

found by now, it will never be found. My guess is that the skull showed the cause of death and he made damn sure that it would never be found. The small bones he assumed would never be found anyway, but only assumed. With the skull it was a real belt and braces job. Surely that points to his guilt?'

'Oh, it does.' Tony Myers, the CPS solicitor nodded in agreement. He was a slightly built man with a pencil-line moustache. He wore a dark suit, a university tie, a white shirt. 'It all points to his guilt. In my heart of hearts I think he murdered the woman ... but can we prove it? The answer is probably not.'

Yellich sighed.

'Well, let's look at it from his point of view. No, no, I don't mean that, I mean let's look at his story and see if we can find a hole in it. His wife, his first wife, falls in the home, cracks her skull ... so an admission of head injuries ... might be a way in. He panics ... their marriage has been in difficulty. He fears being suspected of her murder and so disposes of the body. He was a butcher, he knows how to eviscerate a carcass, he knows how to butcher it, whether bovine or human. I would think the method is the same. He got rid of the flesh and the organs and burnt them. Whatever remained he scattered in woodland where predators would have found them.'

'Christmas came early for a few badgers and foxes.' Another growl from Yellich that caused Hennessey to cast him a disapproving look.

'Whatever ... the bones he boiled to remove the last vestiges of flesh and kept sans skull in a container, he says, about as large as a small suitcase. Would that be all that was required, Dr D'Acre?'

'Oh, yes ... yes.' Dr D'Acre nodded. 'If the bones were cut down and if the head ... the skull, complete with the jaw was removed, then yes, I could fit it in my black bag and have room to spare.'

'Very well. Then, years pass, Mrs Golightly is never more than a missing person. He doesn't benefit from her death, no insurance policy for example.' Myers paused. 'Now, can we prove murder? We all know what we believe, but can we prove it to a jury, prove beyond a reasonable doubt? And I have to say, that in the absence of a confession, it is highly unlikely that we can. We none of us believe him, but we know he can turn on the charm when he wants to. Women on the jury swayed by his allure, especially when he can present himself as a grieving widower; men on the jury who've had quarrels with their wives themselves who can imagine being in the situation he portrays ... We'd be running a risk, hoping the jury could see past that. Further, given the fear that the great and the good upstairs have of unsafe convictions, I think the best we can hope for is convicting him of unlawful disposal of the dead. The judge will likely realize what happened and hand down the maximum penalty, but that still means he'll be a free man in less than four years.'

Hennessey and Yellich glanced at each other. Hennessey and Dr D'Acre avoided any eye contact at all.

'Sorry, but that's it.' Myers opened a palm. 'If you come up with something that proves murder, then we'll look at it again, but with what you've given me, the only safe conviction is...'

'Unlawful disposal.' Hennessey finished the sentence for Myers. 'I suppose we still have the option of charging him with murder later on if new evidence comes to light.'

'We probably ought to cut our losses,' Yellich suggested. 'A bird in the hand and all that ... we get him for something ... he becomes known to us ... it gets him in the system, and as Mr Myers says ... if in the future...'

Hennessey leaned forward. 'No.' He glanced at the table top. 'No ... let's not be defeatist ... I think we can pull victory from the jaws of defeat here.'

'Try a little publicity,' Myers suggested. 'We have one victim that we know of, there may be more ... there might be someone out there who escaped his clutches. If they can come forward...? He's at home, I believe?'

'Yes. We released him without charge on Saturday.'

'All right, re-arrest him. Charge him with unlawful disposal, ask the magistrates for remand pending trial, and make a press statement. Name him. Name his victims.'

It was Tuesday, 9th June, 10.47 hours.

'Not a happy bunny, boss,' Yellich said in response to Hennessey's question. 'Not happy, but still confident, though arrested, cautioned and charged with unlawful disposal of the dead, as Mr Myers suggested.'

'Press release?' Hennessey cradled the steaming mug of tea in his hand. Even on a hot day, like that day, tea was the only drink to drink, in his opinion.

'Went out a.s.a.p., made the breaking news on the regional news slots.'

'Good, good. Well, let's hope we can trigger an alarming memory or two. We'll go and talk to him now, lean on him a bit ... but first...' he picked up the phone and dialled a four figure internal number, 'I saw a Citroën C4 earlier this week, silver, middle-aged man and a younger woman.'

'Oh, yes?'

'Probably nothing in it. As I said to my lunch companion, it won't be the only one in the Vale, but I'll see who it belongs to, anyway. Didn't look like an axe murderer, but they never do. Ah, collator, I have a vehicle registration number for you. Can you find the identity of the owner please? No, I won't wait; I have an interview to conduct. Message in my pigeonhole will suffice.' Hennessey replaced his phone and smiled at Yellich. 'Well, shall we go and chat to Mr Golightly?'

The two men stood and with Yellich walking behind and to one side of Hennessey, they made their way from the CID corridor to the interview rooms. Hennessey opened the door of Interview Room One.

'I'm getting used to this room.' Golightly forced a smile as Hennessey and Yellich entered.

'Don't say anything unless you have to.' The thin man turned to Golightly. 'In fact, my advice to you is to reply "no comment" to every question.' The man then stood and nodded to Hennessey and Yellich. He wore a brown three-piece suit with a gold hunterchain looped across his waistcoat. He was tall, very tall, in excess of six foot, thought Hennessey. 'Short,' he said.

'Sorry?' Hennessey responded.

'Short. My name. Short.'

'Short.' Hennessey echoed, just managing to conceal a smile.

'Yes. Of Grayon, McDonald and Plowright, standing in for Courtney Smyles. Representing Mr Golightly under the terms of the Police and Criminal Evidence Act 1985.' He wore subtle aftershave.

'Very good, thank you, Mr Short. Please be seated, sir. I am DCI Hennessey and this is DS Yellich.'

The four men sat at the square table, Golightly and Short facing Hennessey and Yellich. After the tape recorder had been switched on and the formalities of self-identification completed, Hennessey spoke. 'Mr Golightly, you have been arrested and charged with the unlawful disposal of the dead. This follows the positive identification of the bone fragments found in the concrete apron of the premises once owned by you, as being those of Mrs Rosemary Golightly, your first wife. Do you wish to comment?'

'Please ask a question, Mr Hennessey.'

Short spoke softly, yet with an air of authority.

'Do you know how the bone fragments got there?'

'We have been over this, last Saturday. I told you, I put them there.'

'Mr Golightly...' Short turned to Golightly.

'It's all right, sir.' Golightly showed a deference to the solicitor he hadn't shown to the police. 'I want to get this off my chest, as I said to the duty solicitor last Saturday ... it's all I can do.'

'Very well.' Short turned to Hennessey. 'The charge is unlawful disposal of the dead. That is admitted. Murder is denied.'

'Understood.' Hennessey nodded. 'But if we uncover fresh evidence, we will be pursuing other charges, including murder, if we can.'

'And we understand that.'

'Good. So, Mr Golightly, tell me the circumstances of your wife's death.'

'It was an accident.'

'Yes?'

'We were in the workshop. She slipped and

fell, fell down a set of metal stairs. Died instantly.'

'You are medically qualified to assert that, are you?'

'No, no medical qualifications, but you don't need to be a doctor to tell when someone is dead. No pulse, see, no breathing ... then after a while the skin gets clammy to the touch. That's what it was like with her.'

'So why didn't you call an ambulance or the police?'

Golightly shrugged.

'Please answer ... for the benefit of the tape.'

'No reason ... panicked, I think.'

'Why should you have panicked? If what you say is true, you had no reason to fear prosecution.'

'I wasn't thinking. I panicked.'

'You invite suspicion on yourself.'

'I can cope with suspicion.'

'You even reported your wife to the police as being a missing person, knowing all the while that she was deceased, knowing all the while where her remains were. That is another offence we'll be charging you with.'

'What?'

'Wasting police time.'

'Ha!' Golightly snarled his derision.

'So, what did you do with the body?'

'Laid it out, left it for two days, that lets the blood set solid. Less mess.'

'OK.'

'Then I butchered her. Dismembered the body. Removed what flesh and muscle that I could ... comes off the body quite easily, if you know how.'

'And you know how?'

'Make no secret of it. I'm a butcher by trade.'

'Yes, all the skills and all the tools.'

'Took the flesh and left it in the wood behind the workshop, scattered it about and made sure I was well off the path, dog walkers use the path. The foxes and badgers would have made short work of it. The entrails, well, those I burned then buried.'

'Buried?'

'In the flowerbed by the side of the concrete apron. Doubt if there will be anything left now.'

'We'll check. It will be good for your first

wife's family and your son to have something to bury, a grave to visit. What does young Terence think about this?'

'He thinks his mother walked out on him ... on us.'

'And when he knows the truth? What then?'

'Well ... then ... then I don't know what he'll think. Dare say he'll be angry with me for not telling him the truth, but you know ... the longer you keep the truth hidden, the harder it is to expose it.'

'Not really bothered, are you?'

'About what?'

'About what your son will think when he hears the story of his mother's disappearance.'

'Well, he's a man now, he's old enough to understand.'

Hennessey paused. Golightly's coldness, his absence of remorse ... he and Yellich and Short were in the presence of a very dangerous individual. He continued. 'What did you do with the bones?'

'I told you last Saturday.'

'Tell us again.'

'Cut up the skeleton, sawed it up and put the bones in boiling water, kept it simmering all day. After that the bones were pretty well free of flesh and sinew. Emptied the water onto the waste ground beside the workshop and let Mother Nature take care of the bits of flesh. The bones I sawed up and kept in a sack under some bricks behind the building.'

'How long were they there for?'

'About two or three years.'

'So young Terence was pining for his mother, and all the while she was in a sack behind the workshop?'

'Her bones were, she was in a better place.'

'What did you do with the head?'

'That went into the Ouse.'

'Whereabouts?'

'Off Lendal Bridge.'

'In the middle of York?'

'Yes. Late at night, of course.'

'Oh, of course.'

'It will be well lost by now.'

'Dare say it will ... twenty years.'

'Yes. Where is this going?'

'It's up to me to ask the questions, Mr Golightly ... but since you ask ... where it is going, is that the bones of your first wife lay unconcealed for two years before you decided to conceal them.'

'Nearer three, and they were not lying, they were in an old canvas holdall outside the workshop, anybody that came snooping round wouldn't give it a second glance. Hidden in plain sight is, I believe, the expression.'

'So then, you decide to conceal them in a layer of concrete?'

'Yes ... well, I was selling the workshop, wasn't I? Had to tart the place up, so I decided to lay a concrete apron and on a whim I concealed the bones in the concrete.'

'Fortunately for us.'

'Fortunately?' Golightly's eyes narrowed.

'Yes, because we found them. I mean, if they were bones, just bones, which they were, all you needed to have done is thrown them into the river. If you had done that they would never have been found and you wouldn't be sitting here.'

'Strange you didn't do that,' Yellich added, 'given the manner you disposed of the skull.'

Golightly glared at Hennessey, then at Yellich, and then at Hennessey again.

'Well.' Hennessey spoke as if he enjoyed the sight of the man being consumed with self-reproach. He envisaged Golightly spending many hours in a prison cell thinking, 'If only, if only.' 'You'll be charged with unlawful disposal of the dead. You'll be detained in custody overnight, you'll appear before the magistrates in the morning and we will oppose bail.'

'I didn't believe a word of it,' Hennessey sipped his tea, 'but I didn't particularly expect to.'

'Do you think we could make a charge of murder stick?' Yellich glanced out of the window of Hennessey's office. The walls, the tourists, the blue sky. 'I still think we should just go with unlawful disposal of the dead … it's a waste of time to attempt anything else.'

'And I tell you again, this is my call, not

yours.' Hennessey's jaw was set firm. 'We can and will get more than a conviction for unlawful disposal of the dead out of this one ... Golightly isn't going to walk as freely as he thinks.'

'How are you going to do that?' Yellich pointed to the window of Hennessey's office. 'Look ... that's called a city. People live in a city ... crimes are unsolved because we ... you insist on chasing a rainbow.'

'I am not chasing a rainbow!' Hennessey's face flushed with anger. 'There's a murder conviction here and I am going to get it ... with you or without you, Yellich, but I am going to get it. I'd prefer you to be with me ... but ... a transfer might be appropriate.'

'You really think that will solve the problem ... leave you to work alone?'

'I'd prefer to be alone than have a DS who isn't with me one hundred percent.'

'I am capable of support, you know that ... but it's qualified. You're going down the wrong road ... there's other cases out there ... still unsolved ... we're wasting our time with Golightly ... win some, lose some. That's the way I see it.'

'Well it isn't how I see it! Make a decision Yellich, you are with me or you are not ... I am happy either way.'

Nicole Butterworth had been drinking since midday. She had been sitting alone in her tenancy in Tang Hall, soaking up daytime television, nursing a hangover, when the midday news was broadcast. There was little that interested her. She watched the news like she watched soap operas or American comedy shows. It was just something to watch, something that, unlike her life, was neat, clean, well ordered, non-threatening. She cared little for the Bank of England base rate being lowered, or the state of the European Union, or the outcome of the trial that was allegedly gripping the nation, because it did not grip her: all impinged minimally on her world. Her world was her flat and her walk to the shops. All she cared about was whether it was raining or not. Then the Regional News was shown and that man, him ... he appeared ... those eyes ... and it all came flooding back. She longed for the gin bottle. There was a little left, just a little, enough to give her that fateful taste. She knew that once she had the taste, then that was it ... she'd go to her death. She'd been dry for two months ... she was on the way to getting on top of it, but those eyes ... she didn't care. She remembered why she drank. Drink was never a failing with her until her path crossed that of that ... that ... thing ... that monster. Afterwards it was her only comfort. She sank the contents of the bottle, then reached for her purse and opened it. She'd been paid ... her dole had come through on Saturday morning, a fortnight's money. She could blow the lot very easily. She didn't care about how she would survive until the next Giro. She stumbled out of the door, more through shock than the effect of the gin. She took a bus into the town and walked into the first pub she saw. She ordered a double gin and tonic. It was expensive, and soon she was drinking fortified wine. Both her parents had been alkies and both had died of liver failure. She remembered them sitting on the couch in the cold and damp council house in Sheffield, talking with harsh, rasping voices and her father saying, 'It's the quickest way, Nicole, the quickest way out of Sheffield is through a pub door.'

She had moved on from her parents' life, from Sheffield and from their lifestyle until she met ... him. Then the demon awoke in her, as though it had been in her blood all along. She fought it, became dry again and just happened to watch the midday news...

She drank until the barman, in a kindly tone, said, 'I think you've had enough, pet. Time to go home.' She didn't protest but turned meekly and teetered towards the door. Outside the world was harsh, the sun bright and high. She walked up Micklegate towards the Bar, the gateway to the ancient walls ... to the police station opposite the bar. Collecting herself she walked up to the enquiry desk and said to the youthful constable. 'It's that man ... that man on the television ... Golightly. He tried to murder me once...'

It was Tuesday 9 June, 14.30 hours.

Nicole Butterworth focused on the mug of black coffee. 'I need this but I don't want it.'

'I quite understand.' Hennessey spoke kindly.

'Do you?'

'Well, I think I know what you mean.'

'Have you had a drink problem?'

'No, but I am a police officer, long serving ... we don't get paid much but we see life. I have met many alcoholics.'

'I was doing so well. I was off it for two months.' She spoke slowly but she was sobering quite rapidly. Her speech was not at all slurred; she seemed to know where she was.

'Drink your coffee,' Hennessey urged.

'Plenty more where that came from,' Yellich added. 'Have you eaten?'

'No, not yet. Just a slice of toast at breakfast.'

'Hungry?'

'Yes ... a bit.'

'A lot, more like.' Yellich stood. 'I'll see what I can rescue from the canteen.' He left the interview room.

'He's a nice man.' Nicole Butterworth smiled as she raised the beaker of coffee to her lips.

'DS Yellich?' Hennessey smiled, 'Yes, he's a good egg. I'm lucky to have him as my sergeant.' He did indeed feel that he was lucky to have Yellich. He found himself warming to the man once more after the recent 'ice age'. 'So, do you want to tell me about Terence Golightly?'

'Him … that monster … he tried to murder me.'

'Start at the beginning.'

'Well, it was about three years ago. We met at the "New World".'

'A pub?'

'A nightclub. It's shut now. Nightclubs don't have a long life expectancy. But we met, we drank, had a dance … I mean, I have always thought that any relationship that starts when the couple meet each other at a nightclub is bound to fail. I mean, what have any two people got in common if they met at a nightclub, except that they are lonely?' She shook her head. 'Never thought I'd go into one, but … well, I was desperate … that emptiness inside that comes from needing someone. So I went. He chatted me up and bought me a drink. We met a couple of days later, by arrangement. We seemed to talk to each other all right. So one thing led to another and we became an item.'

'He was married.'

'Yes. Told me he was divorcing her. Probably wasn't true but you tend to believe what you want to believe. We met at my house.'

'On Tang Hall?'

'Yes ... small one-person flat, really cramped ... like a rabbit hutch. Anyway, he started to show the other side of his personality. He was a control freak. I could do this, but not this, and we were not even married. I was all for getting out but he had this way of holding on to me. I mean like head games.'

'Yes ... I have come across the like before.'

'Long service police officer, I bet you have. You must meet all sorts.'

'We do. All sorts of good and all sorts of bad ... but do carry on.'

'Well, it was summer ... like this ... hot and dry and he wanted us to do "it" in the open, he said he'd never done that ... he fancied it. I tried to persuade him that it's difficult, it's quite hard to do it in the open, it's uncomfortable and you are always scared someone will see you, but Terence gets what he wants, when he wants it. So off we went in his car ... middle of the afternoon, mid-week. He was self-employed, he said, so he had that flexibility ... he could have been employed and was stealing time from his employer, either could have been true. So we drove to the country and found a small wood and we did it, it wasn't a good experience but he got what he wanted, he'd done it out of doors at last.'

The door of the interview room opened and Yellich appeared holding a plastic container. 'BLT,' he said, 'it's all they had left.' He handed it to Nicole Butterworth.

'It'll do.' She tore open the package. 'Thanks, I didn't realize how hungry I was until you mentioned it.'

'You've arrived at the right time,' Hennessey said as Yellich resumed his seat. 'Nicole and Mr Golightly have just made love in a wood, this was three summers ago.'

'Ah...'

'Yes,' Nicole Butterworth swallowed, 'and then he grabbed me, really tight ... told me he was going to kill me ... really calmly, really matter of fact. I was scared. I mean, I was thirty-three years old ... not a lassie but not an old woman either ... plenty of time left. He said, "I've done it before ... not for a long time, but I've done it and I want to do it again. It's like a hunger ... once you get the taste ... once you know you can do it and get away with it." He said that's why he'd brought me to the wood, it wasn't just for sex, it was to kill me.' She put the sandwich down.

'All right, take your time.'

'It's hard to talk about it.'

'In your own time...'

Nicole Butterworth chewed the sandwich. 'Well, he said he knew how to get rid of a body, he said he butchered it, removed all the flesh from the bones. He said he left the flesh and innards out for the foxes, the bones he sawed up and boiled, except the skull. The skull he dropped in a river. He told me he murdered his first wife. He said his wife annoyed him so he smashed her over the head a few times with an iron bar. He said he had to get rid of the skull because it was fractured ... like, in many places, he said he couldn't claim it was an accident if the skull was found.'

'Go on ... this is good.'

'Very good,' Yellich added.

'This will help you?'

'Oh, yes...'

'Anything to keep that monster off the streets.'

'So what happened?'

'He said he laid an apron of concrete. I don't know what is meant by an apron of concrete, an apron is what I wear when I do the washing up ... but he said "apron".'

'And that's what he did ... we found the bones.'

'So it said on the news this lunchtime. How does this help you then?'

'His admission of murder, that's what we need.'

'But it's only my word...'

'With everything else we've got, it ought to tip the balance in our favour.'

'Really?'

'Yes, really. So what happened then?'

'Well, I struggled. He had his hands round

my throat ... I groped for something to hit him with. I found this rock and hit him on the side of the head. He fell back looking stunned ... sort of angry that I dared to do that, so I hit him again and caused a gash over his left eye ... then I ran ... picked up my clothes and ran.'

'You didn't report it?'

'For what purpose? His word against mine. He didn't bother me after that ... just left me alone ... but then I started to drink, like, heavily ... it was how I coped ... then I came off it, then this lunchtime I saw he'd been arrested so I took a drink and got the taste and it was when I was in the drink in the pub that I decided to come here and tell you what happened three years ago.'

'We are very pleased you did.' Hennessey paused. 'If you'd let Mr Yellich here take your information in the form of a statement ... I have a visit to make, excuse me.'

Hennessey stood and left the interview room and walked to the stairs. He went down the tiled echoing stairway to the cells and asked the custody sergeant to be allowed into the cell in which was held Terence

Golightly. He found Golightly sitting on the single bench, propped up against the wall.

'Four ... out in two.' Golightly smiled. 'And that's the maximum, my lawyer told me. So it could be even less, could be three, out in eighteen months.' Hennessey thought he looked smug. 'You know, I could get

used to it ... three meals a day, medical care ... I can see positives already. I'll miss the women and the beer, but two years inside won't be the end of my life. Maybe I'll even learn a few things...'

'Nasty-looking scar you've got on your forehead, Terence.' Hennessey held eye contact with him. 'We've just been talking to Miss Butterworth.' Hennessey enjoyed watching the colour drain from Golightly's face, watching his jaw sag, his eyes widen. 'Interesting incident in that wood three summers ago ... It's a more convincing explanation for trying to hide the bodies than you "panicked". It means your fear of prosecution for murder was well grounded. Two years...' Hennessey shook his head. 'I don't think so ... twenty more like. Have a nice day.'

Hennessey returned to his office via the enquiry desk and his pigeonhole. He had two messages, one notifying him of a party to celebrate the promotion of an officer whom he knew and who worked in a neighbouring division, and the other was a note from the collator advising that he had got 'a result' on the Citroën C4 query. He walked on to his office and picked up the phone on his desk and dialled a four figure internal number.

'Collator.' The voice at the other end of the line was brisk, efficient.

'DCI Hennessey. I got your note ... you have information for me?'

'Yes, sir. The Citroën C4 you asked about ... it is registered to one Dr Albert Maudsley of Great Whitley'

'Great Whitley, where is that?'

'Out in the Vale, sir.'

'Thanks, I'll look it up.' He replaced the receiver and reached for the file on the murder of Mary Golightly and added the information to the recording. 'Maudsley,' he said, closing the file. 'Where? Where? Where? And a doctor ... where?'

On an impulse he picked up the phone again, dialled nine for an outside line and then, consulting the file, he dialled the number for Gravely Health Centre.

'Dr Maudsley is out for the afternoon,' said the helpful voice of June March. 'Do you want to make an appointment, sir?'

'No, thank you,' Hennessey replied softly. 'It doesn't matter. Thank you.'

She was cold. Even in the heat of summer, she was cold. It was a different kind of cold ... it was cold brought on by fear. Here in the dark, in the cellar ... locked in ... chained to the wall. She tried to calm herself. While she was alive, Julie Orr told herself, while she was alive ... then there was still hope.

It was Tuesday, 16.45 hours.

Seven

Tuesday, 9 June,
16.50 hours – Wednesday, 15.30 hours
in which a second arrest is made and a middle-aged couple find poignancy.

The realization hit Hennessey with an impact that was tangible. He sat bolt upright in his chair then leaned forward, hand on forehead. 'Yellich!' he shouted as he reached for the phone on his desk. He was rummaging in his jacket pocket and jabbing a four figure internal number as Yellich stood, a little woodenly, and with a show of reluctance, in his office doorway. 'Ah, Yellich ... a Citroën.'

'Yes, sir.'

'C4...'

'Yes, sir...'

'I saw ... Ah, collator, please.' He held the

phone away from his ear.

'I saw him abduct a girl.'

'What!' Yellich became alert, more animated. 'You saw...'

'Maudsley ... it's just struck me. Earlier this week ... I was having a late lunch ... I saw Maudsley. I knew I'd seen him somewhere ... but that was it. You're right, Yellich, my memory is going a bit – but the instincts are still there!'

'I never said—' Yellich began to protest.

'Oh, never mind, never mind, you've have been right if you did. I'm sorry I've been snapping at you all week, I've just been worried about getting past it ... But this is it, I know we're right this time. So let's just bring him in, you and me, yes?'

Yellich looked at him for a moment, then gave a grin of relief. He was about to say something when Hennessy started speaking into the phone again.

'Ah, collator, DCI Hennessey here. Do we have a mis per report on a young adult female reported a few days ago? We do? Can you have the file sent up to me? Yes, a.s.a.p. Thanks.' He replaced the receiver. 'It's

Maudsley.'

'Maudsley from the health centre at Gravely? Good God.'

'I wrote his car number down ... just an old copper's instinct. Still there, Yellich, still there! I saw him with a young woman ... she looked bowled over by him, such is the kudos of the medical profession. Ah, yes...' He checked the details on his pad. 'Strange.'

'What is, boss?'

'His home address is given as being in Brookman's Park.'

'Where's that?'

'Hertfordshire.'

'Down London way?'

'Yes ... north of London.'

'He must have just moved up ... in the process of changing address.'

'It's the only explanation. Look, get onto the police at Potters Bar, they'll cover Brookman's Park. If they don't they will know who will. Ask them for anything they have on Albert Maudsley ... his numbers put him at fifty-four years of age. Then you and I will go back out to Gravely.'

Thirty minutes later, after an uneventful

drive across the flat lush landscape that is the terrain to the east of the city of York, Hennessey and Yellich entered the sombre, quiet, but not completely silent, health centre at Gravely.

'Good morning, Mrs March.'

June March looked anxiously about her. 'If you want any other information...'

'It's all right.' Hennessey held up his hand. 'The information you gave was excellent, helped us indeed...'

'Oh...' June March flushed with pride. 'I saw on the news that you had arrested him, but it only said unlawful disposal of the dead.'

'There will be other charges.'

'Will there?' she whispered.

'Oh yes, but that's between you and me. Tell me, is Dr Maudsley here?'

'No, he phoned in sick today ... we are a doctor short, fortunately we are not busy...'

'I see. How long has he been with this practice?'

'Just joined us ... a matter of weeks. He joined us from a practice in the south ... he's a nice man, he says he's still getting used to the climate up here ... the long summer evenings, the short winter days.'

'I know what he means, I'm a Londoner from Greenwich ... I go back when I can. So, what is Dr Maudsley's home address?'

'I don't know.'

'It's critically important, June. A matter of life or death.'

'Literally,' added Yellich.

Both men then sensed a feeling of unity that had been lost over the last few days. It was, they both felt, like meeting an old friend.

'Well, in that case...' June March reached forward and tapped on the computer keyboard. 'He's in Elmton,' she said, 'Nine Vicarage Lane, Elmton.'

'Elmton?'

'About five miles away ... that direction.' She pointed eastward.

'Thanks.'

Hennessey and Yellich drove to Elmton, Yellich at the wheel. Hennessey, holding his mobile to his ear with one hand, writing on his pad with the other, said 'Thanks,' and closed his mobile and slipped it into his pocket. 'Hate those things, but there is no denying their use, clearer reception than the radio. Anyway, anyway ... smoke without fire.'

'Sorry, boss?'

'The Hertfordshire boys do know Albert Maudsley ... as an un-convicted rapist.'

'Oh ... really?'

'Yes, really.' Hennessey paused. 'Apparently, some years ago he was prosecuted for rape but the case collapsed. The judge stopped the proceedings halfway through the trial ... this was at St Albans Crown Court. He ... the judge, ordered the jury to return a verdict of not guilty by direction. It was the old story of her word against his. She said rape ... he said it was consensual. No corroborative evidence on either side. She ... the victim, didn't make a particularly credible witness by all accounts, she was of good character, but was tearful and timid in the witness box. He, by contrast, was calm and assured. After the trial he said he thought his reputation and name had been sullied so much that he couldn't go on living in his ... and I quote, "beloved Hertfordshire", and intended to seek to join a practice elsewhere in the UK. The case never made national news.'

'I see ... and so he ends up in our patch, for our sins.'

'Yes ... and once in our patch he becomes associated with a lady whose leg was found in a refuse bag ... but there's more.' Hennessey tapped his notebook.

'Oh?' Yellich briefly glanced to his left.

'Yes, there was a twenty-five year old woman who was a known associate of the good Dr Maudsley ... one Monica Atkins.'

'Associate, sir?'

'They apparently had a liaison ... then it cooled ... but Ms Atkins is friends of a female police officer who met Dr Maudsley socially, just prior to his trial...'

'Interesting.'

'Oh yes, wheels within wheels ... and it was this officer who gave us the information. Anyway, her intuition was that Maudsley was as guilty as sin, but as she said, you can't present intuition as evidence. Anyway, Hertfordshire CID are going to fax all they have on Albert Maudsley up to us.'

'Good.'

'Like trying to nail jelly to the wall...'

'Sorry, boss?'

'That's what the female officer said of Maudsley ... trying to get hold of his personality was like trying to nail jelly to a wall.'

'Colourful turn of phrase she has ... but it describes a slippery customer.'

'Indeed. She also said that "he can charm the birds out of the trees ... but only to kill them". They are very interested in developments up here.'

'I can imagine.'

'And they are going to try to link him with unsolved disappearances down their way. It's all falling apart but we still have no evidence. Anyway, press on Yellich, please ... that girl...'

'Miss Orr, Julie Orr.'

'She might still be alive.'

Nine Vicarage Lane, Elmton, revealed itself to be a very typical doctor's residence. It was of the same black and white half-timbered 'L' shaped design that was the style of Louise D'Acre's house in Skelton. A police mini bus containing six white-shirted constables, two of whom were female, and a sergeant, stood outside the address.

'Good, they're here,' Hennessey observed; a little unnecessarily, thought Yellich.

Yellich halted the car behind the mini bus. The uniformed officers got out of the mini bus as Hennessey and Yellich got out of their car.

'Force entry, please.' Hennessey addressed the uniformed sergeant in a calm but authoritative manner.

The house was clean and neat and tidy inside. There were a few books to soften the interior, but those that were on the shelves were arranged so that those with the tallest spines were on the outer edge of the shelf, so that the line of books dipped mid-shelf. The magazines on the coffee table were arranged from left to right in alphabetical order. The garden, as viewed from the house, had a regimented look, being closely maintained to the point that Hennessey thought that it seemed oppressed.

But there was no Julie Orr. Every room, every cupboard, was investigated. The house was searched from basement to rafter.

'Garden?' Yellich suggested, and Hennessey nodded to the uniformed sergeant, who led his crew out into the garden.

'Can't tell you how many I've done ... I don't know myself. Strange that you ... that I could lose count.' Albert Maudsley sat in the armchair looking at the shivering, trembling, whimpering Julie Orr. 'Strange, really, such a momentous thing it is to take a human life, you'd think I'd remember ... but I don't ... they seem to blend into one another. Dare say people would say I'm mad ... but to me it feels normal ... so very normal ... but I do like to spend a little time with the victim before ... well, before the end. I like to explain ... or maybe not explain because you know, truth to tell, I don't know why I do it. Really. I like the power ... I do feel a sense of power ... but that's not the "why" of it. I mean, if I really wanted power, I'd make them suffer ... I'd probably prolong it ... but I won't, Julie ... I won't ... I promise ... it will be quick ... you won't feel anything, a bang on the head ... enough to knock you out ... or even semi-conscious, it will be like being in a dream for you ... after that it's really simple ... a plastic bag ... best murder weapon ever invented ... over your head ... you suffocate but because you will be unconscious or at least semi-conscious, you won't experience that awful panic ... then ... then ... well, it's just a question of waiting. I'll wait for two days; your blood will be congealed by then ... after that I'll lift your body onto the workbench ... you'd see it to your left if I removed the blindfold ... and the bow saw ... the sort of saw a woodsman would use to cut branches off trees ... carpenters' saws don't do the trick ... not enough bite to get through human bone ... then parcel up the bits in more plastic bags ... and ensure that each bag is weighted, is punctured so it will sink and ensure that all bags are disposed of. I made a mistake there ... heard the thing rolling round in the back of my car, put it in a wheelie bin ... ought not to have been discovered, but it was ... that was the only mistake I ever made. I should have turned round and made sure it went over the bridge with the rest of her, but I didn't. I won't make the same mistake with you though ... just finish this coffee.'

Maurice Walls, intrigued by the police activity in the neighbouring house, left his study and walked out into the garden and leaned on the fence that separated the properties. He caught eye contact with the older of the two plain-clothed police officers. You?' he called.

'We are looking for Dr Maudsley.' Hennessey raised his voice, enabling it to carry across the width of lawn and the flowerbed which separated the two men.

'Aye ... if he's not at work and not at home, you'll likely find him at his lock-up. Imagine, all this garden and he still wants a lock-up ... knew a bloke once ... had a garden as big as this...'

'Where's the lock-up? Maudsley's lock-up?'

'Far end of the village ... right at the end of the road ... line of lock-ups ... garages on the left, can't miss them. His is the one with the yellow doors.'

'Sergeant!' Hennessey turned and called to the uniformed sergeant.

'Sir!'

'Back in the van! Lock-ups ... look for a silver Citroën ... follow myself and Mr Yellich ... sharply!'

Two hours later Hennessey and Yellich sat in Hennessey's office.

'That's going to haunt me.' Yellich glanced out of the small window at a group of gaily-dressed tourists walking the walls, clutching guidebooks and cameras.

'I know what you mean.' Hennessey looked down at his desktop. 'A matter of seconds ... we'd have caught him, he wasn't going anywhere, but another few seconds ... and that bag would have been over her head.' Hennessey paused. 'Well, I don't normally do this, usually I wait until just before last orders after taking Oscar for a walk, but I feel like making an exception. Would you care to join me for a beer?'

'Love to, skipper,' Yellich smiled, 'love to. In fact I know just the place ... real beer, quiet, not crowded at this time of day.'

Epilogue

Both trials took place at York Crown Court the following February.

Terence Golightly's trials were short, lasting just over five minutes apiece. He pleaded guilty to the murder of Rosemary Golightly, guilty to the rape of Nicole Butterworth, and offered no defence or plea in mitigation. He was sentenced to two consecutive terms of life imprisonment.

Albert Maudsley, by contrast, pleaded not guilty to the abduction, rape and false imprisonment of Julie Orr and not guilty to the murder of Mary Golightly. He smiled charmingly at the jury throughout his trial. Only upon being found guilty did his demeanour change, and he was dragged snarling from the dock, having also been sentenced to life imprisonment, but with the recommendation that he serve a minimum of twenty-five years before being considered for parole.

Nicole Butterworth continued to visit the small wood where 'it' happened, doing so on a near-weekly basis, feeling stronger and more in control of herself after each visit, and more importantly, managing to keep herself free of alcohol.

At the end of February, a few days after the trial of Albert Maudsley, a silver-haired man and a short-haired woman some years his junior stood side by side, arm in arm, on the hill overlooking the Marine Drive at Scarborough. A fierce, cold east wind tugged at their clothing as they watched the blue-green sea heave and crash against the shore, while to their left, the Corner Café stood empty, the open air swimming pool was closed, and the line of beach huts deserted, all under scudding grey clouds.

'I always find something poignant about a resort town off season,' Louise D'Acre observed.

'Yes,' Hennessey replied after a pause. 'Yes, there is. Poignancy is the word.'

φ